QUEEN VICTORIA'S POTTY

Toilets run in W. C. Flushing's family.
His gran, the formidable Dame Netty
Flushing, was a tireless campaigner for
a public convenience in every town.
It was she who inspired his lifelong
love of lavatories. 'Thanks to Dame
Netty,' W. C. Flushing recalls fondly,
'my entire life has been toilets.'

- -

W. C. Flushing is best known for
his great ten-volume work,
Our Toilet Heritage.

Dedicated to my gran,
Dame Netty Flushing,
whom I shall always put on a pedestal

'No writer can equal W. C. Flushing
in full flow' – *Times Toilet Review*

SUPERLOO

QUEEN VICTORIA'S POTTY

W. C. Flushing

Illustrated by Martin Chatterton

PUFFIN

PUFFIN BOOKS

Published by the Penguin Group
Penguin Books Ltd, 80 Strand, London WC2R ORL, England
Penguin Group (USA) Inc., 375 Hudson Street, New York, New York 10014, USA
Penguin Group (Canada), 90 Eglinton Avenue East, Suite 700, Toronto, Ontario, Canada M4P 2Y3
(a division of Pearson Penguin Canada Inc.)
Penguin Ireland, 25 St Stephen's Green, Dublin 2, Ireland (a division of Penguin Books Ltd)
Penguin Group (Australia), 250 Camberwell Road, Camberwell, Victoria 3124, Australia
(a division of Pearson Australia Group Pty Ltd)
Penguin Books India Pvt Ltd, 11 Community Centre, Panchsheel Park,
New Delhi – 110 017, India
Penguin Group (NZ), 67 Apollo Drive, Rosedale, North Shore 0632, New Zealand
(a division of Pearson New Zealand Ltd)
Penguin Books (South Africa) (Pty) Ltd, 24 Sturdee Avenue, Rosebank,
Johannesburg 2196, South Africa

Penguin Books Ltd, Registered Offices: 80 Strand, London WC2R ORL, England

penguin.com

First published 2007
1

Text copyright © Susan Gates, 2007
Illustrations copyright © Martin Chatterton, 2007
All rights reserved

The moral right of the author and illustrator has been asserted

Set in Monotype Baskerville
Typeset by Palimpsest Book Production Limited, Grangemouth, Stirlingshire
Made and printed in England by Clays Ltd, St Ives plc

British Library Cataloguing in Publication Data
A CIP catalogue record for this book is available from the British Library

ISBN: 978-0-141-32007-6

CHAPTER ONE

'Every rescue mission we go on,' complained Finn, 'I seem to be dressed in coal sacks!'

He was standing inside a toilet – the kind of automatic, self-cleaning public loo you find now in many towns. From the outside, it looked like a silver space-age pod. It had flashing signs: FREE, BUSY, CLEANING. Inside it was all shiny, streamlined metal. It had all the usual things: toilet bowl, hand-washing station, jumbo bog-roll dispenser.

But this was no ordinary public loo. This was *Superloo*, a toilet genius with a giant-sized computer brain. Superloo had many amazing talents. For a start it could talk. And it could travel back in time.

At this very moment, it was getting ready to whizz off to Victorian times where, with its friend Finn, it planned to rescue one of its toilet ancestors and bring it back to the twenty-first century.

'These trousers itch like mad,' moaned Finn.

From a grille in the cubicle ceiling came Superloo's quacky robot voice. 'Never, ever, say the word *trousers*,' it warned him, 'when we go back to Victorian times!'

'Why not?' asked Finn.

Superloo's other friend, Mr Lew Brush, popped his head round the cubicle door. 'Because trousers are *unmentionables*,' he said.

'Yeah, Superloo just told me.'

'No, Finn, you don't understand,' said Mr Lew Brush. '*Unmentionables* is the Victorian word for trousers. The real word was just too rude. Ladies and girls would swoon clean away!'

'For heaven's sake,' muttered Finn. But he wasn't surprised. Victorians were so easily shocked. Hadn't they even covered up piano legs?

'So what *can* I talk about?' Finn asked.

'Best stick to jelly,' Mr Brush advised him. 'That shouldn't offend anyone. The Victorians were jelly mad. It was Queen Victoria's favourite pudding, if I'm not mistaken.'

The toilet genius butted in. It hated not being the centre of attention, even for just two minutes. 'I can't wait to meet my toilet relative,' it burbled.

Finn and Mr Brush exchanged glances. They both knew how much its relatives meant to Superloo. Those ancient loos were primitive, yes, with not a brain cell between them, but to Superloo they were family.

And Mr Lew Brush, a lifelong toilet fanatic, was as keen as Superloo to see this particular loo – the famous 1812 Overture Toilet.

'I'm looking forward to it too,' he told Superloo. 'Victorian times were the Golden Age of toilets. Think of the great Thomas Crapper! Think of those ground-breaking toilet designs: the Niagra, the Rocket, the Deluge! But the 1812 Overture Toilet,' and here Mr Brush's voice dropped to an awed whisper, 'that loo is a *legend* in toilet circles. Only one was ever made.'

It was made by Sir Walter Closet, Mr Brush's all-time toilet hero, as a gift for Queen Victoria. Sir Walter had been a toilet manufacturer in this very town, back in the nineteenth century.

'For its time it was quite revolutionary,'

quacked Superloo. 'A daring experiment! It had the most powerful flush of any Victorian toilet. It could suck down ten ping-pong balls! And it was the first loo to play music when sat upon.'

'And not just any old music,' added Mr Brush, 'that rousing battle tune *The 1812 Overture*, with cannon fire!'

'Of course,' quacked Superloo, as if everyone should know, 'the purpose of such loud music was to drown out any rude noises. Victorians were really embarrassed about being heard on the toilet.'

'That's why they invented potty baffles,' Mr Brush pointed out.

'*Ahh*, yes!' enthused Superloo. 'Potty baffles! Weren't they like big lacy doilies, with beads round the edge?'

'Spot on!' cried Mr Lew Brush. 'A simple device but ingenious. You just draped one over your potty. Then peed *through* it, so muffling any rude tinkling sounds! In fact, I have one right here in my pocket! Would you like to see it, Finn? A genuine Victorian potty baffle? Don't worry, I rinsed it out in the sink.'

'Err, thanks but no thanks,' said Finn hastily.

'Look, can we get back to my trousers – I mean, my *unmentionables*. This brown colour is disgusting. Don't tell me, I bet I'm dressed as a peasant again.'

'You're a Victorian street urchin,' Superloo corrected him smugly. 'Actually, it's a brilliant disguise. To Victorian toffs, servants and poor people were practically invisible. And brown is the most sensible colour. Because many street urchins had jobs to do with poo.'

'Oh great,' muttered Finn, wondering as he said it why he'd promised to go with Superloo on its latest time-travelling trip. After every trip he said, 'No way! I'm never going again!' But, always, the silver-tongued toilet persuaded him.

'Yes!' Superloo was raving. 'You could col-lect dog poo, for instance. Some poor people shovelled up dog poo for tanners – if you were really poor you didn't even have a shovel. Or be a street sweeper, who swept up horse dung . . .'

'Look,' said Finn through gritted teeth, 'I'm *seriously* having second thoughts about this trip . . .'

Suddenly the toilet's pompous voice changed. It became pathetic and pleading.

'Oh, *pleeeease*, Finn,' it begged. 'I had such a brilliant plan.'

Finn sighed again. Superloo always had *brilliant* plans. The trouble was, they so often went pear-shaped. He said, 'I don't want to hear it.'

But Superloo was telling him anyway.

'About one hundred and forty years ago,' it started, 'Queen Vic passed through this town in her royal train. She was off to Balmoral, her Scottish castle, but she stopped here briefly to receive the gift of the 1812 Overture Toilet – presented to her in gratitude for a magnificent bronze statue of Prince Albert that she had given to the town.'

'Statue?' Finn found himself saying. 'Of Prince Albert? Is that the guy on that horse in the town square? The one all splashed with pigeon –?'

'As I was saying,' snapped Superloo, annoyed at being interrupted, 'the 1812 Overture Toilet was at the station . . .'

Then it seemed to break down again. It always got emotional about its toilet relatives, especially the famous ones used by royalty. 'But that's the last record of it,' Superloo lamented. 'After that, it just vanishes from history. Did the Queen take it away with her? Or didn't she? Even my vast databanks can find no trace of it.'

'There, there,' soothed Mr Brush. 'Don't upset yourself.'

But now the toilet was talking through choking sobs. 'My p-p-poor relative,' it raved hysterically. 'Lost in the mists of time! Abandoned! Forgotten!'

'For heaven's sake,' Finn shouted. 'I'll come with you. Right? I'll wear these *unmentionables*. Only, just stop crying!'

He hated it when the toilet cried.

'Hey, great,' boomed the toilet cheerily, its mood changing instantly now that it had got its own way. 'Victorian times, here we come! Set time-travel coordinates for the town railway station. *Toodle-ooo!*' it warbled to Mr Brush. 'We'll be back before teatime.'

It slid its cubicle door shut.

A muffled shout came through the door: 'Finn? If you get the chance, could you get me another potty baffle? It'd make my day!'

'I'm going to pretend I never heard that,' Finn decided.

Grim-faced, he clung to the toilet bowl. He'd never get used to time travel. The ceiling lights flashed. The cubicle began to rotate, slowly at first then faster, faster.

'Blast off!' shrieked Superloo. Finn's world became a silver blur.

'*Aaaargh!*' he yelled as the centrifugal force snatched him off the toilet bowl and spread-eagled him on to the smooth, shiny walls.

Mr Brush would never get used to time travel either. He had never been with Superloo on one of its rescue missions. He always stayed behind to take care of things in the twenty-first century. But, even from the outside, it looked weird. One second Superloo was here – a great silver cubicle, big as a telephone box. Next it started to shake, like a washing machine on fast spin. Then twirl into a glittering silver cyclone. And then *WHOOSH!* it was gone, leaving scattered stars behind it.

Mr Brush stood alone in the shed on his allotment where he and Superloo had been living.

'Wish I could go with them,' he murmured.

He would have loved to meet his hero, Sir Walter Closet, but someone had to stay behind to keep an eye out for Superloo's enemies.

'Those toilet hunters will never give up,' he told himself.

Not until they'd got their hands on that microchip. The four-billion-dollar one from NASA that had been put into Superloo by mistake. It had made an ordinary loo into a time-travelling genius, but its real purpose was to make spaceships leap through light years, reach distant planets in minutes. Whoever had it could conquer the universe. As a result, there were many people desperate to get their hands on Superloo's brain.

Mr Brush glanced out of the window. He saw other ramshackle sheds like his, rows of peas and lettuces, dusty gooseberry bushes. There was nothing suspicious. Only the big green van that emptied the allotment wheelie bins. Superloo's brain seemed safe, for the moment. But he knew he had to stay alert.

The green van trundled along the lane. The wheelie bins were in a neat row outside the allotment gate. It hoisted each up in turn, emptied them, put them down again. Then it rumbled away.

Mr Lew Brush checked his watch. *Better get a move on*, he thought.

He glanced outside again. His faithful blood-hound, Blaster, was sniffing around among the pea sticks. Every few seconds, his sad baggy face looked back anxiously at the shed.

Mr Brush waved through the window – 'I'm here, boy!' – to show Blaster he was OK. The old dog got really upset if he was parted from his master, even for a minute.

But, sometimes, Mr Lew Brush had to go out. Like he did this morning. So he resorted to his usual trick. He had a dummy of himself, a sort of scarecrow, dressed in his old duffle coat. He heaved it into his chair. It had a cabbage for a head and straw stuffing bursting out of the coat.

Mr Brush put his old fishing hat on the cabbage. It wouldn't have fooled a baby. But it was enough to fool Blaster, who was half blind and not too bright. The crumbling old hound came tottering in. Mr Lew Brush crouched behind the chair.

Blaster wheezed over, sniffed at the duffle coat, slobbered on the scarecrow's twiggy fingers. His dear old master wasn't dead, was he? A faint tooting sound came from Blaster's rear end. It always got leaky when he was stressed.

'It's all right, boy, I'm just having a snooze,' Mr Brush said from his hiding place.

The old hound's tail wagged feebly. Satisfied, Blaster staggered off to his basket and settled down. Soon he was asleep, twitching, dreaming of the days when he used to chase rabbits.

Mr Brush crept from behind the cabbage-head dummy. Quietly, he gathered up his banner. It said SAVE OUR ALLOTMENTS on it. He hadn't told Superloo yet, but their little home was in danger. The council wanted to sell the allotments to property developers. They would bulldoze the sheds and build 'exclusive, executive homes'.

If they did that, where would he and Blaster live? Where would Superloo hide out from its enemies?

Mr Brush tucked Blaster's tatty blanket round him, so the old hound didn't get cold. Then he tiptoed out and shut the shed door behind him.

With his banner under his arm, he set off for the bus stop. He was going to the town square to protest on the steps of the town hall.

After Mr Brush had gone, all was peace and quiet on the allotments. Blaster snored in his basket. The only other sound was the twittering of sparrows in the gooseberry bushes.

Suddenly the lid of one of the wheelie bins lifted up, very slightly. A pair of cruel, glittering eyes peered out from the darkness inside. They flickered around. Then, very softly, the lid dropped again.

CHAPTER TWO

'Slavey!' screeched Miss Gripper. 'Are you listening to me?'

'Beg pardon, miss?' said the slavey.

The slavey was kneeling by the drawing-room fire. She was supposed to be stoking it with coal, but she was swaying with weariness. There were deep purple shadows under her eyes. A slavey was the lowest of all the Gripper servants, at everyone's beck and call. She scrubbed and polished and dusted all day. Her hands were cracked and sore. And her arms were nearly torn out of their sockets from lugging coal and hot water up four flights of stairs.

Miss Gripper was lounging on a sofa, scoffing jelly from a crystal dish. She was dressed from head to toe in the richest clothes, all pretty frills and flounces, but her face was mean and spiteful.

'I said, did you polish that coal before you brought it up from the cellar?'

Young Master Gripper was dressed in a red velvet jacket and knee breeches. His golden locks were curly. His cheeks were pink. He looked like an angelic child. Except for his eyes, which were sly and weasly.

'It doesn't look very shiny to me.' He scowled. 'I shall tell Ma of her and she will get a thwashing!'

When Master Gripper got excited and especially when he talked about violence, he never could pronounce his Rs.

'Did you iron Pa's newspaper?' demanded Miss Gripper. 'And his bootlaces?' Her pa was Lord Gripper, of Gripper's Superior Chamber Pots.

'S-sorry, miss.' The slavey trembled. 'But I have not had time yet.'

'Then you should get up earlier,' scolded the priggish Master Gripper.

But the slavey had been working like a dog since five o'clock. She'd crept down in the dark from her tiny attic bedroom, carrying her boots so she didn't make a sound. Even the other servants weren't up this early. Her bare feet had scrunched on cockroaches in the kitchen.

They went scurrying in all directions. Her first job was to light the big iron kitchen stove, then take the cook a cup of coffee. And when the Gripper family woke up, it got really busy. They were always ringing bells from their rooms, wanting this or that.

Brrring! Brrring!

'More hot water here, slavey!' roared Lord Gripper.

Brrring! Brrring!

'Pass me my shawl, slavey,' twittered Lady Gripper, too lazy to reach out and get it herself. 'No, not that one, you noodle, the other one!'

Brrring! Brrring! The slavey could even hear those bells in her sleep.

The two odious Gripper offspring were dressed in their fanciest clothes. This afternoon, they were going with their parents to the railway station to see Walter Closet's sensational new invention, the 1812 Overture Toilet, presented to Queen Victoria.

'*La!*' screeched Miss Gripper, throwing down her jelly spoon and bouncing up from the sofa. 'Pa was raving most dreadful about that Walter Closet this morning. I thought he would bust a blood vessel!'

Lord Gripper was a bad-tempered bully at the best of times. But Queen Victoria's visit had put him into a rage. 'It should be a good, honest Gripper chamber pot that they present to Her Majesty!' he'd roared as he left for his factory after breakfast.

'Indeed, Lord Gripper,' Lady Gripper had snootily agreed. 'That they should have chose that Walter Closet above you! It's a scandal! He was nothing but a common gardener's boy.'

She seemed to forget that Lord Gripper himself came from humble beginnings. That, before starting his own business and making a fortune, he'd been a barrow boy, flogging potties door to door.

'That upstart! He shall learn that no one makes a fool of Lord Gripper. By God, I'll shoot him down like a rat or a mad dog!'

He'd glowered around him, his face dark with fury. Then he'd crammed on his top hat and gone stomping out to his magnificent carriage, with four horses and two tall footmen in scarlet-and-gold livery.

'Out of my way!' he'd snarled to a servant scrubbing the steps of Gripper Towers. And, 'Whip them horses – I'm late!' he'd growled to the driver as the great carriage went rumbling down the drive.

'I would like to see Pa shoot down Walter Closet,' said the angelic Master Gripper with a nasty gleam in his eye. 'I weally, weally would. There would be wivers of blood!'

'*Pooh*, you booby!' said the ferret-faced Miss Gripper. 'Pa don't mean to actually shoot him. But, if I know Pa, he'll find some way to ruin him.'

The slavey, whose name was Rosetta, was kneeling by the fire, polishing coal on her sleeve. Miss Gripper gave her a kick with her sharp-toed, button-up boots. 'Was you listening, slavey? You slyboots! You should not listen in to the conversations of your betters.'

'I weren't, miss,' murmured Rosetta, keeping her head low. She knew better than to provoke the Gripper children. They took after their pa. There was nothing they liked better than bullying servants and making their lives a misery.

But Rosetta had been listening. And her heart gave a leap of fear. She would always be grateful to Walter Closet. He had been very good once, both to her and her big brother, who was a chimney sweep's climbing boy. She would hate to see anything bad happen to Walter Closet, but she knew that Lord Gripper was rich, powerful and cruel. Anyone the potty magnate saw as a rival was ruthlessly crushed.

Rosetta could feel the awful Miss Gripper breathing down her neck, just waiting to pounce, like a cat with a mouse. Miss Gripper was only eleven, the same age as Rosetta, but the Lord's daughter could get the slavey sacked on the spot. And Rosetta desperately needed this job. Her family depended on her now Ma had died and Pa couldn't work since his accident.

'Use the tongs, slavey!' snapped Miss Gripper. 'We don't want the dirty hands of a *common* person touching our nice clean coal.'

'Or I shall tell Ma!' squealed Master Gripper, who was a terrible sneak and telltale. 'And she shall have you thwashed!'

The snooty Lady Gripper came sweeping into the room. She was all dressed up to see the Queen. Her bustle made her bum seem as big as a wheelie bin and she clanked with jewellery. Her best hat was decorated with two dead birds of paradise, their beautiful tail feathers trailing down and their glass eyes peering over the brim.

'Children, I have a most frightful headache,' she wailed, collapsing on to the sofa and wafting herself with a huge ostrich-feather fan.

'Slavey, ain't you done yet?' said Master Gripper in his shrill, peevish voice.

Rosetta stood up in her coarse blue dress, apron and big clumpy boots. Something creaked.

'*Ohhh,*' groaned Lady Gripper dramatically. 'That sound cuts right through my head.'

'It is the slavey's fault,' said Miss Gripper gleefully. Rosetta felt all their vicious little eyes staring at her. She swallowed hard.

'Is it your knees, slavey? Or your boots?' taunted Miss Gripper.

'No, miss, I swear,' said Rosetta. 'I oiled my boots this morning.'

'Perhaps it is your corsets then,' smirked Miss Gripper.

'Then she must oil those,' moaned Lady Gripper feebly from the sofa. 'I cannot abide a creaky corset.'

'Well said, Mama,' declared Master Gripper. 'Slaveys should not cweak. Or they should be whipped! Slaveys should be silent. And inwisible.'

Rosetta was trembling now. She felt like a lamb surrounded by wolves. Had they finished with her yet? Or did they want to torment her some more?

But then, suddenly and unexpectedly, she was saved by Lord Gripper. He had come back from the factory. He came bursting into the room. He didn't even notice Rosetta, but she daren't leave without permission. She crept into a corner near the door and hid herself behind some heavy velvet curtains.

'My lady!' bellowed Lord Gripper. Lady Gripper turned pale. The children stood to attention, like little soldiers. Everyone – his factory workers, his servants, even his own family – was terrified of Lord Gripper.

But the bullying old brute seemed to be in a good mood. He was smiling for once, but that made him even more scary. His smile showed two eye teeth, as long and sharp as wolf fangs.

'I have something to show Your Ladyship,' he said. And he took, from behind his back, a potty and held it out to her.

'My Lord?' said Her Ladyship, puzzled.

She'd seen loads of potties before. Lord Gripper's factory churned out thousands of them. He didn't approve of the newfangled flush toilets. 'Common folk are too stupid to use 'em,' he'd thunder. 'All they need to pee in is a plain, simple Gripper's pot!'

'Look, look inside it, woman!' roared Lord Gripper, thrusting it in her face. 'I've had five hundred of 'em specially made. They'll ruin that upstart Walter Closet, or I'll eat my hat!'

Still looking bemused, Lady Gripper stared into the chamber pot. Lord Gripper's factory was famous for its rather rude novelty potties. Some had an eye in the bottom and the words I SEE YOU! Some had the face of Britain's old enemy Napoleon in them. You could even, for a price, order a personalized potty. With a picture of your worst enemy painted inside.

Such vulgar potties might have made Lady Gripper blush. But this one shocked her to the core. She gave a great shriek of horror and fell back on the sofa in a swoon.

'*La!* Ma's fainted.' Miss Gripper shrugged as if she didn't care a penny. She looked into the potty too. But she didn't faint. She was much tougher than her ma, more like her father. Instead, she gave a delighted giggle at what she saw inside.

'See!' said Lord Gripper, turning the potty upside down. 'I've stamped Walter Closet's name on the outside, so everyone will think he made 'em, and, when the Queen arrives, my men will give 'em away free to the crowd.'

Everyone knew that Lord Gripper had a gang of hired thugs, ex-convicts and bare-knuckle fighters, to do his dirty work for him.

Miss Gripper clasped her hands joyfully. 'I declare, Pa, it's a brilliant plan! There'll be a riot!'

'And *wivers* of blood,' said the ghoulish Master Gripper.

'And Walter Closet will be ruined,' said Lord Gripper, clenching his fist tight, as if he were crushing the toilet inventor inside. 'He'll make no more dratted musical toilets. He'll be locked up, most likely, sentenced to hard labour.'

'You can make sure he is, Pa, since you're the magistrate,' grinned Miss Gripper.

'*Egad*, a girl after my own heart!' roared her proud pa, clapping her on the back, his two pointy wolf teeth glinting. 'And listen, you two.

My men have particular orders to make sure that everyone, gentry as well as common scum, gets a free potty. So when you get your pot, Miss Gripper, I want you to make a big fuss. Your ma will faint, of course. That's all she's good for.'

'Don't worry, Pa,' said Miss Gripper, who was sharp as a knife. 'We'll play our part. I shall shout, "Treason! This is a plot against the Queen!"'

'Better and better,' said Lord Gripper, delighted.

'And I shall shout, "Constables! Awwest Walter Closet!"' said Master Gripper shrilly, waving his arms about.

Lord Gripper suddenly stopped smiling. From under black, bushy eyebrows he gave his children a savage glower. 'You'd better play your part well,' he threatened them, 'for I want to be rid of this Closet upstart for good and all.'

He went stomping out of the room.

Everyone had forgotten Rosetta, trembling behind the curtain. She slipped out of the door, unnoticed, carrying her empty coal bucket.

She began the weary trudge down to the kitchen.

'Where've you been, girl?' shouted the cook, as soon as she saw her. 'Them rabbits needs skinning! And them jelly moulds needs polishing. I want to see my face in 'em, mind!'

Rosetta said meekly, 'Yes, Cook.' But she was thinking about Walter Closet and how she could get word to him of Lord Gripper's fiendish plan. What was it about those potties that was so shocking? Rosetta hadn't a clue. But it was something that would lead to the toilet inventor's downfall – to him being thrown in the clink and made to tramp on a treadmill or grind bones up for fertilizer.

'Wait,' whispered Rosetta to herself. She had an idea. Her brother was in the house some-where. He'd been brought here today by Mr Bains, his master, to give the chimneys of Gripper Towers a good clean.

If I could find him, thought Rosetta, *he could warn Walter Closet.* But where was he? Probably up a chimney somewhere, scraping out soot.

And how could she search for him? She had rabbits to skin and jelly moulds to shine. And Cook kept a beady eye on her all the time.

Rosetta sighed. The copper jelly moulds hung in a row on the wall. She took one of them, shaped like a castle, and began to polish it.

'Perk up, girl!' said Cook sharply. 'Use some elbow grease! When *that*'s finished, I wants you to go to the cellar and fetch me more coal for the stove.'

CHAPTER THREE

Whump! Superloo seemed to have landed.

Finn slid off the wall into a crumpled heap. He staggered dizzily to his feet.

'Where are we?'

'According to my time-travel calculations,' quacked Superloo, 'we have landed at the railway station. In the lost-property office, to be precise. We are hidden behind a heap of top hats and parasols.'

It slid open its cubicle door a few centimetres.

Superloo didn't have eyes, but it didn't need them. The sensors built into its body told it all about its surroundings. It even had an electronic nose to sniff out smells.

'My sensors detect there is no one else here,' it informed Finn. 'It's all perfectly safe. If you step outside, you'll see through the window the bustling town station. And great steam trains thundering in, like iron monsters, hissing, steaming, sending out showers of sparks!'

'Cool!' said Finn, carried away for the moment by Superloo's poetry. 'But where's this 1812 Overture Toilet?'

'In this very room,' said Superloo smugly, 'waiting to be moved out on to the platform, ready for the Queen's arrival this afternoon. The dear old Queen,' burbled Superloo. 'She wasn't a load of laughs, but she cared for her subjects. Did you know she donated her very own bloomers to hospitals, so poor people could wear them? Not many people know that.'

'What, like, *after* she'd worn them?' Finn shuddered. 'If I were a poor person, I'd say, "No thanks!"'

But this was no time to discuss Queen Victoria's bloomers. He had a toilet to find. And it all sounded quite straightforward. 'You mean I don't have to go outside this room?' he asked Superloo. This mission sounded easy-peasy, really well planned. They'd be back home before teatime!

'You're a genius!' Finn told Superloo.

'I know,' said Superloo smugly.

'Only problem is, how do we get your toilet relative inside this cubicle?'

'Oh, that's easy-peasy too,' said Superloo breezily. 'You forget, I'm a hoverloo now.'

In between trips, Superloo was forever complaining that it could travel through time, but that once it arrived it was stuck in one spot. So Mr Lew Brush had tried various things to make it mobile. None of them had worked very well, but Mr Brush's latest wheeze was a big rubber airbag fixed to Superloo's base. Now Superloo could skim along like a hovercraft. It could control everything, inflating and deflating the bag, speed and direction, from inside its computer brain. Unfortunately, this air-filled cushion had one little design fault . . .

But Superloo didn't want to think about that now. It was too excited. Its famous toilet ancestor was just metres away!

'I'll just hover right over to it,' Superloo told Finn, 'and then you can push it through my cubicle door. If it's too heavy there are bound to be trolleys lying around. Anyway, we'll work something out! I'll just inflate my hover cushion . . .'

'Wait!' said Finn. 'Don't you think I'd just better go outside and see if the 1812 Overture Toilet is actually here?'

'Of course it is,' said the toilet huffily. It slid its door open wider. 'Go and check it out.'

'What's it look like?' asked Finn.

'Well, legend says it was magnificent!' gushed Superloo, almost in ecstasies. 'With a golden chain and a mahogany seat and a fine porcelain bowl shaped like a crouching lion! The music came crashing out from a phonograph hidden in the cistern. But, of course, to be presented to the Queen, the whole affair had to be hidden inside a wardrobe.'

'A wardrobe?' said Finn, baffled.

'Well, it would be far too shocking for her to gaze upon an actual toilet. The Victorians liked to pretend they didn't exist. They put their potties into piano stools, sewing boxes, even bookcases. They called going for a pee *going to pluck a rose.*'

'Is it just me,' asked Finn, 'or were Victorians really weird?'

He stepped outside, looking for a loo disguised as a wardrobe. His heart was beating wildly, like it always did when he left the safety of Superloo. Meanwhile the great toilet genius was all systems go, its sensors on red alert. If this was a railway station, where were the rumbling train wheels? That bonfire smell of flying sparks?

'*Whoops*,' yakked Superloo. 'I think I've made a slight miscalculation.'

At the same time, Finn yelled back, 'It's really dark out here! There's no top hats or parasols. No wardrobes either!'

'So where are we?' said Superloo, its super-confident voice crumbling a little.

The only light came through Superloo's half-open door. Finn peered into the gloom. Were they in a cave?

Shiny black heaps towered all around him. He tried scrabbling up one, but small rocks slithered from under him, clattering to the floor. He'd started an avalanche!

'*Aaargh!*' He slid back to the bottom in a hail of black lumps. His face was smeared, his clothes filthy.

'What's happening out there?' called Superloo helplessly.

Finn picked up one of the lumps, inspected it, stared around him again at the dimly spar-kling piles.

'I think,' he told Superloo, 'we're in a coal

cellar. Turn up your cubicle lights so I can see better.'

But Superloo didn't have time because, suddenly, high up near the ceiling, a door burst open. Light flooded on to a flight of steep, stone steps. Then Rosetta came clumping down with an empty bucket.

She didn't see Superloo, hidden behind a coal heap. But she did see something move in the cellar's dark corners. She saw gleaming eyes. Was it a rat?

She rattled her coal bucket. 'Go away, you nasty varmint!'

Then she made out a boy, coal-blackened from head to foot: his face, hands and clothes. 'Snake!' she said, surprised. 'Snake, is that you? It's me, Rosetta.'

She'd known her brother was somewhere in Gripper Towers, cleaning the chimneys. She hadn't expected him, though, to be down in the coal cellar.

'Where is your master – Mr Bains?' she whispered. Mr Bains usually kept a very close eye on his climbing boys in case they ran away.

She looked around fearfully, but her brother seemed to be alone.

Several coal heaps separated them. She began clambering over to get closer to her brother, but then Cook's angry bellow came from above.

'Slavey! Get up here this instant. You ain't gutted these rabbits!'

Rosetta looked fearfully back up the stairs. 'Coming, Cook!' she shouted.

'Snake!' she hissed. 'Cook's on the rampage. I ain't got much time. Just listen! Lord Gripper, the villain – he's out to ruin Walter Closet. You remember Walter Closet? How kind he were?'

This time, Finn had the sense to nod. He'd been frozen with panic before, too startled to run and hide. But now that he saw it was a girl, a thin, weary girl about the same age as him in great clumsy boots, his racing heart slowed a little.

She was telling him something in a low, urgent voice.

'Snake, you must warn Walter Closet! This afternoon, when Queen Victoria comes, Lord Gripper's a-going to give out chamber pots that are supposed to be made by Walter Closet but ain't really. And these fake potties, they makes ladies faint – I didn't see why perzactly.

But they do! And Miss Gripper says they will cause a riot! And Walter Closet will end up in prison because of them!'

'Where are you, you wretch?' yelled that fierce voice again. 'I shall box your ears!'

'I must go!' said Rosetta, scooping up some coal in the bucket. Then she dashed off. Halfway up the stairs she turned and hissed down into the shadows, 'You must warn him, Snake. He is in great peril.'

Then the cellar door slammed shut and it was dark again. Superloo's lights beamed out and made the coal heaps glitter. They showed Finn the way to safety. He rushed back inside the silver cubicle. The toilet genius slid its door shut. Finn leant against it, panting.

'Did you hear that?' he gasped. 'She said Mr Lew Brush's hero, Walter Closet, is in great peril! Some kind of evil potty plot! We have to help him!'

CHAPTER FOUR

'We can't get involved,' insisted Superloo again. 'Our mission is – rescue my relative, the 1812 Overture Toilet. Then we're out of here.'

Finn couldn't believe the great toilet genius was going to leave Walter Closet to his fate – to be set up by the evil Lord Gripper, put in prison, fed on bread and gruel, even flogged with a cat-o'-nine-tails.

'Mr Lew Brush will never forgive us,' said Finn.

But still Superloo pompously insisted, 'This is not our concern!'

Usually Finn was patient with the brainy bog: its whims, its sulks, its bossiness. It must be tough, being a genius trapped inside a toilet body. But Finn was feeling quite stressed him-self at the moment. Who wouldn't be, on these time-travel trips? He burst out in an explosion of anger; he just couldn't help it: 'You're so selfish. You don't care about humans at all. All you care about is smelly old ancient toilets!'

Superloo was silent.

Is it in a huff? thought Finn. *Have I hurt its feelings?* It hated anyone being rude about its toilet ancestors. But, for once, Finn just didn't care.

At last, Superloo spoke. And it said something totally unexpected.

'Do you really think I'm such a heartless monster, Finn?'

It sounded wounded, and disappointed. 'Look, you've got it all wrong. The *reason* I don't want to get involved is it's too dangerous. Dangerous for *you*. Lord Gripper isn't a man to tangle with. He's a gangster. If you get in his way, he'll trample over you.'

Superloo was full of surprises. It seemed that, for once, it wasn't thinking of itself. 'You're my friend, Finn,' said the toilet simply. 'I'd hate anything to happen to you.'

Finn was touched. And, strangely, it didn't seem at all weird having a toilet as a best mate. He was embarrassed now by what he'd said before. 'I'm sorry,' he apologized. 'I thought, I thought . . .'

'Never mind that now,' Superloo chipped in, its voice suddenly bright and chirpy again, 'because my brilliant brain has solved the problem. You can go and warn Walter Closet, but I'll go with you, to protect you. What do you think of that?'

'*Errr*, yeah, great,' muttered Finn. But he was full of doubts. Wouldn't he be better off on his own as a street urchin blending in? Wouldn't having a silver twenty-first-century public convenience hovering beside him make him rather conspicuous?

'Hang on,' said Finn. 'Open the door.'

Superloo slid its door open. In the glow of its cubicle light, Finn gazed around the cellar. 'How are you going to get out of here?' he asked the toilet genius. 'There are coal heaps all around you, and then those narrow stairs –'

'I'm aware of that,' interrupted Superloo in its know-it-all voice. 'My scanning radar has already informed me.'

'Even if you get to the stairs and can hover up, you're too big to fit through that door at the top.'

'I'm working on it now,' said Superloo, its brain whirring.

'But we haven't got time,' said Finn.

Superloo huffed and puffed, but it had to admit that Finn was right. The digital clock on its wall showed 8.00 a.m. Victorian time and the Queen was arriving at three o'clock this afternoon. If there was any chance of foiling the fake potty plot, Walter Closet must be told as soon as possible.

'And your batteries won't last forever,' warned Finn. Whenever they time travelled, the great toilet genius had to rely on stored supplies of electricity.

'Yes, all right, all right,' said Superloo testily. There was nothing for it. Finn would have to go alone, but first the toilet had a little weep. 'On the sidelines again!' it sniffled. 'Left behind!'

'For heaven's sake,' said Finn, who had no time to sympathize. 'You're the controller! The mastermind! Without you we wouldn't be here at all.'

'You're right!' said the toilet, all bouncy again.

It forgot its self-pity and got down to business. 'Right now, Walter Closet is at the railway station, putting the finishing touches to the 1812 Overture Toilet,' it informed Finn. 'He's such a perfectionist! I've got a map out of my databanks. It's of this town in Victorian times. Anyway, you go out of Gripper Towers, turn left –'

'I know where the railway station is,' interrupted Finn. At least on this trip he was on familiar territory. In his own town, even though it was almost 140 years ago.

'If I find a way out, I'll meet you there at the railway station,' said Superloo.

That horrified Finn. 'No, stay here!' he begged. 'Then I'll know where to find you.'

Superloo was his ride home. If he lost the toilet, he'd be stuck in history forever. Every time-travel trip, he panicked about that.

'Oh, all right,' huffed Superloo.

'You promise?' asked Finn. He knew how stubborn the toilet could be, how reckless it was once it got an idea in its head.

'I just wanted to be part of the action for once,' sighed the toilet.

'There isn't going to be any action,' said Finn. 'I'll just warn Walter Closet. I'll come back. Then we go straight home. OK?'

'OK,' said Superloo like a sulky child. But then, instantly, it seemed cheery again. 'If you come across my relative, the 1812 Overture Toilet –'

'Look, I'll do my best,' said Finn. Although, privately, he didn't have much hope. Even if he did find the legendary loo, how could he get it back to the coal cellar, and without anyone noticing?

'Thank you, Finn,' said Superloo gratefully. Finn was surprised it wasn't making more fuss. He knew how much its toilet ancestors meant to Superloo. Maybe the great toilet genius had resigned itself. Maybe it knew too that it was hopeless, that it would have to leave this relative behind.

'I'm going now,' said Finn.

So why didn't he? His mind kept telling him there was no time to waste, but his feet seemed reluctant to move. He forced them to step out of the cubicle door.

He stood there shakily, looking around. He started scrambling over the coal heaps and climbed up the cellar steps. Very quietly, he opened the door at the top and peered out into the kitchen of Gripper Towers.

He couldn't see Rosetta. She was plodding upstairs again – Miss Gripper had rung for more jelly. The cook was at a big scrubbed table. She had her back to him. Her sleeves were rolled up, her brawny arms dusty with flour. She was knocking seven bells out of some bread dough. Even from the back she looked tough, like she could wrestle a grizzly bear.

Finn could see the back door beyond her. If he could reach that, he would be free. Hardly daring to breathe, he began to creep round the kitchen. He left sooty handprints on the white walls and black boot prints on Cook's clean floor.

He was almost there! But Cook had eyes in the back of her head. Suddenly a muscly arm shot out and grabbed Finn's ear.

'*Gerroff!*' yelled Finn.

He struggled but Cook was too strong. She twisted his ear.

'*Ow!*' Finn hollered. 'That hurt!'

But Cook didn't let go. She seemed as wide as a bus; she could crack walnuts with those fingers. And she was in a foul mood.

'What are you a-doing of?' she screeched. 'You dirty wretch! Just look at this mess! You climbing boys should be up chimneys! Not in the clean kitchens of decent folks!'

And she dragged him by the ear, protesting all the way, upstairs and into a cluttered parlour. There was a jungle of potted ferns, forests of furniture and knick-knacks.

'Look out, you clumsy clodhopper!' yelled
Cook as Finn's elbow almost knocked a vase
off the piano.

Now they were standing in front of a huge
fireplace. 'Good,' panted Cook, puffed out
from all those stairs. 'The fire ain't lit. You can
start here.'

'Start what?' gasped Finn.

'Cleaning the chimneys, of course. Why do
you stare like that, you dunderhead!' raged
Cook. *'Lawks a mussy!* I've got pies ready to
come out the oven. Now get up there. Or I'll
give you such a crack!'

Finn stared at Cook, with her furious red
face, jigging about in anger. He didn't have
much choice. He shot up the chimney.

There was a little ledge just inside. He
squatted on it like a frog, waiting for Cook to
go. But she was wise to that.

'I'll set this fire going!' she shrieked up the
chimney. 'Then you'll soon shift!'

Panicking, Finn hoisted himself further up.
At first there were four iron rungs to climb,
like a ladder, but then they ran out, and he
was all alone in the sooty dark.

Afterwards, Finn would never know how he
made it up that chimney. It was sheer fright.

Every second he thought he could smell smoke and feel heat from the fire Cook had threatened to light. He was wedged in the chimney, in a sitting position, his back braced against one side, his boots on the other. And somehow, in a mad, desperate scramble, he shuffled upwards, walking his feet up the chimney wall and digging in his elbows, using them as levers. He wouldn't have thought he had the strength. Sometimes, there were sticking-out bricks to use as handholds and footholds, taking the weight off his trembling limbs. And all the time he was coughing, breathing in soot and scared to death that he might tumble into the flames below.

'No! Don't fall!' screamed his panicking brain. 'They'll take you to hospital! Put you in a pair of Queen Vic's smelly old bloomers!'

Desperately, he clung on, hoisted himself a bit further up.

Suddenly a feeble ray of sunshine fell on his fingers. Finn looked at it wonderingly. He raised his sooty, sweat-streaked face. Above him there was a tiny square of blue sky.

I've made it! thought Finn.

But he hadn't noticed that the chimney was getting narrower. That he was being squeezed until his knees were braced on the wall instead of his feet. That his arms were clamped tight to his sides. He tried to make that final push up to light, freedom and fresh air, but he couldn't. He was stuck fast, like a cork in a bottle. He couldn't even wiggle his fingers.

It was his worst nightmare: trapped in a tight space, in the dark, unable to move or breathe.

'Help!' yelled Finn wildly. 'Help! I'm stuck!'

Only his head could move. It strained upwards towards that blue sky. But his body seemed gripped in a vice.

He gave another forlorn, desperate cry. 'Help! Can anybody hear me?'

A voice above him said, '*Gor blimey!* Don't kick up such a row.'

A grimy arm reached down the chimney. A hand searched around. It grabbed a handful of Finn's hair and pulled.

'Ow!' yelled Finn. The hand found his collar and began yanking on that. And Finn felt himself move, just a bit. He struggled violently.

'Stop twisting about!' commanded the voice from above. 'I got you! Now shoot yer legs out!'

Finn tried to kick with his legs. They suddenly unbent.

'*Aaargh!*' he cried. He thought he was falling back down the chimney, but the arm had him safe. For such a thin, sticky arm it had amazing strength. Finn's collar was almost ripped off his coal-sack costume, but it didn't matter because now his head and shoulders were free of the chimney. Sunlight flooded his face.

One last tug and he was pulled out of the chimney and dumped in a sooty, choking heap on the roof of Gripper Towers.

Meanwhile, in the cellar far below, Superloo was getting restless. It had promised to stay put, but now it was having second thoughts.

'I must get out and find Finn,' fretted the great toilet genius.

Superloo was very fond of Finn. But he was only human, with a poor feeble brain.

'Without my super-intelligence, he could get himself into all sorts of scrapes,' tutted Superloo.

And it had a more selfish intention. As well as helping Finn keep out of trouble, it was determined to rescue the 1812 Overture Toilet.

'My brilliant brain will find a way out of this coal cellar,' quacked Superloo to itself.

It was working on the problem now. Its circuits buzzed, whizzing through possibilities, surfing the Net at lightning speed.

'Bingo!' cried Superloo. On the website of a local history society, it had found what it needed – the original plans for Gripper Towers.

'There's another way out!' the toilet crowed in triumph.

The plans showed a trapdoor, wide enough for Superloo's cubicle. It opened on to the stableyard and, even better, there was a wide ramp leading down from it, for rolling barrels into the cellar.

Perfect, thought Superloo. *I could hover up a ramp, easy-peasy.*

It scanned its surroundings, searching for this new escape route.

'Found it!' quacked Superloo.

The ramp was right where the old plans said, against the far wall, leading up to a big trapdoor. A strange gurgling sound came out of Superloo's speakers. Could it be laughter? Finn would have been amazed because he thought the great toilet genius had no sense of humour.

But it just couldn't help giggling at how gob-smacked Finn would be when it turned up at the railway station and said, 'Guess who? Yes, it's ME!'

Time to inflate my hover cushion, thought Superloo. Its brain sent instructions to the airbag on its bottom.

Its cubicle shot up, and seemed to be wobbling on top of a bouncy castle.

Whoooa! Way too much air, thought Superloo, letting some out. *This hovering lark needs practice!*

It had forgotten about the tiny design fault. As the air whooshed out, it made an enormous trump, like the biggest whoopee cushion in the world.

Oh dear, how rude! thought Superloo, giggling some more as it hovered around the dark, glittering coal heaps towards the ramp.

CHAPTER FIVE

Finn gasped, 'I'm all right!'

Someone was pounding him on the back. He coughed up one last lot of soot, then looked up through red stinging eyes at his rescuer. 'Just don't take me to hospital. OK?'

'I weren't going to,' said the small skinny boy crouching beside him.

He had black bristly loo-brush hair and was even more soot-caked than Finn himself. He had soot in his eyelid creases and inside his ears. But his eyes, flashing in a sooty mask, were bright and lively as a little terrier dog's. They gazed scornfully at Finn.

'Why didn't you buff it?' the boy demanded. 'Then you wouldn't 'ave got stuck. And where's yer scraper?'

'Buff it?' repeated Finn, bewildered. 'Scraper?'

'*Yah!* Ya *are* green,' said the boy, even more scornfully. 'Is this yer first time up a chimbley? Yer *scraper* is what ya scrapes off the soot with. And *buff it* means climbing without yer clothes!'

'Without any clothes?' said Fin, aghast. 'What, not even underpants?' His knees and elbows were already scraped red raw. He cringed to think of the damage if he'd been climbing completely nude.

The boy noticed Finn's bleeding knees. He shook his head and tutted. 'Master'll rub salt in 'em tonight,' he said, 'to make the skin harden. And God help you if you cries.'

Finn, still dazed from his awful experience, staggered to his feet: 'Where are we?'

'Watch yerself!' cried the boy, grabbing him again. Finn blinked the soot out of his eyes. '*Aaargh!*' He'd nearly stepped into thin air. And it was a long way down – a dizzying drop.

They were high up, on the roof of Gripper Towers. The Gripper coach, rumbling down the drive, looked no bigger than a child's toy. It was taking Lord Gripper back to his factory, to supervise the last stages of his potty plan.

'I feel giddy,' moaned Finn.

His rescuer dragged him back to a sheltered spot between the great chimneys.

''Ere, sit down a bit,' he said in a kinder voice. 'Get yer wits back.'

Finn sat, head down, his hands clasped round his knees. The boy who'd saved him was rabbiting on, giving him some useful chimney-cleaning tips.

'When you gets stuck up a chimbley,' he told Finn, 'the worst thing you can do is get all worritted. Them as gets worritted is them as gets smothered.' He tapped his bristly bonce. 'You must keep a cool head. There's allus some way you can wriggle loose. Well, nearly allus.'

His little soot-grimed face became tragic for a second. He was thinking of his friends, climbing boys, who hadn't been able to free themselves. And had no one around to rescue them.

He shook off these dismal thoughts and looked curiously at Finn. The new boy was rather strange. He spoke funny. Maybe he was a foreigner? But that didn't matter – all climbing boys must stick together. You might depend on your mate for your life.

He patted Finn on the back, trying to comfort him. 'I knows what it's like,' he said. 'When I got stuck first time, I got the horrors too. Lor, did I yell! It was Mr Bains as pulled me out and boxed my ears into the bargain.'

At last, Finn lifted his head. 'Thanks,' he said. 'Thanks for rescuing me. I'm Finn, by the way.'

'Pleased to make yer acquaintance,' said the boy, sticking out his hand. 'I'm Snake.'

'Snake?' echoed Finn, as if to say, 'Where'd you get that name?'

But Snake didn't want to talk about that. His nickname came from a past he'd rather forget. He just said, 'I come here to clean the chimbleys.'

Now Finn's brain was clearing, making connections. 'Do you know Rosetta? She works here.'

'My sister – that she does!' said Snake, amazed. 'As a slavey! And hates it too, worse than I hates chimbley climbing. Do you know her?'

'I just met her,' said Finn, 'down in the cellar. She thought I was you. She told me something important.'

And, crouched among the chimney pots, Finn told Snake all about the evil potty plot. How Lord Gripper had made the potties in his factory and stamped them with Walter

Closet's name. How, this afternoon, he was going to give them out to the crowds gathered to cheer Queen Victoria, and how that would cause the most dreadful scandal.

Finn didn't mention Superloo. He knew from experience that you couldn't explain the great toilet genius to someone from another century. Even a twenty-first-century person would say, 'A time-travelling, self-cleaning public convenience? With a brain? Are you completely round the bend?'

When he'd finished, Snake wanted to know the very thing that Finn had been wondering. 'Did Rosetta say why these chamber pots was so shocking?'

Finn frowned. 'She didn't see the actual potty, but she heard Lord Gripper say that Walter would be ruined. That he'd be ruined and put in prison. She said he'd been kind to you.'

'My pa was hurt bad,' explained Snake, 'in an accident in Lord Gripper's factory.'

To pay Pa's doctor's bills and to buy food, Snake and Rosetta had been forced to beg in the streets. Policemen had tried to arrest them; they'd been whipped out of the way by carriage drivers and Walter Closet had dug deep in his pocket and given them two shillings. That was a fortune when you only earned a penny a day as a climbing boy. He and Rosetta would never forget that act of kindness.

Snake didn't tell Finn about the begging. He just said: 'Walter Closet is a fine gentleman – he helped us. We must save him. But how?'

Snake's dirty face wrinkled up, as if he was thinking fiercely.

'Rosetta said we must warn him,' said Finn, 'and I know where he is. He's at the railway station right now, with the 1812 Overture Toilet.'

'Then we must go there!' said Snake, springing up. Finn got up too. With the wind whipping his hair and crows flapping past at eye level, he gazed out over the view.

But where was his home town? He could hardly see it. It was down there somewhere, hidden under a haze of smutty black smoke from factory chimneys. He could see the river flowing into it, but when it came out the other side, it was purple and bright orange! Poisoned by the paints and chemicals from Lord Gripper's potty works.

It was a good job Finn wasn't any closer. He'd have seen other things in the river: a few dead dogs, for a start; the blood and guts from slaughterhouses; loads of floating sewage and bubbles of foul gas, plopping up to the surface and bursting.

'What's that place?' asked Finn, pointing.

On the riverbank, a strange brick building poked up through the smoke. It was shaped like a giant bottle.

'Don't you know nothing?' said Snake. 'That be Big Bertha, the great oven at Lord Gripper's factory, where he bakes his chamber pots.'

He frowned. He didn't like to talk about Big Bertha. It was in that very oven that Pa had had his accident. So instead he said, 'It ain't far to the station from there.'

'How do we get down from *here*?' asked Finn.

He stared around them. The roofs of Gripper Towers, some flat, some sloping, spread in all directions, with a forest of tall chimney pots, twisted like candy sticks.

'I'm not going back down that chimney,' said Finn, already shivering.

'We ain't going to do that,' said Snake. 'Come on. I knows another way, but we must keep a good lookout. We don't want Mr Bains to catch us.'

'Will he be angry?' asked Finn.

Snake shot Finn an astonished look as if to say, 'Is that a *serious* question?'

'He'll send Butcher after us,' said Snake in a shaky whisper. Mr Bains was a cruel master, especially when he was drunk, but Snake was more scared of Butcher. Just mentioning Butcher's name made Snake shudder.

'Who's Butcher?' asked Finn.

But Snake was already scuttling away. He knew these rooftops well. They shinned down drainpipes, balanced along parapets, scrambled down ivy on to balconies. It was a hair-raising journey for Finn. Several times he slipped. He almost went crashing down into the Gripper gardens, crammed with statues and fountains. Snake, however, seemed as surefooted as a mountain goat.

Finn dropped down on to a balcony, breathless, his legs wobbly. 'Where next?' he gasped.

A quick slide down a drainpipe and they were on a wide flat roof. There seemed to be no way down from here. Finn thought, *We're trapped!*

Snake whispered, 'We must go through the house.' He knelt down and prised open a skylight.

Finn gulped. He didn't want to meet that cook again, have his ear half pulled off and be ordered up a chimney. Snake was more scared of meeting Mr Bains and Butcher, but he was pretty certain they wouldn't be inside the house. The last time he'd seen Mr Bains he'd been loading sacks of soot on to his donkey cart in the stableyard.

Snake wriggled through the skylight and Finn swung himself down too.

A soft feathery thing swung into his face.

'*Yurgh!*' cried Finn, batting it away. It was a dead pheasant, hung up by a hook through its neck.

'*Phew!*' Finn covered his nose. There was a strong smell of rotting meat. They were in some kind of pantry. As well as pheasants, dead ducks and hares and rabbits dangled all around.

'*Buzzz!*'

Finn flapped at a fat, shiny bluebottle, trying to land on his mouth. The flypapers, hung from the ceiling, were thick with struggling flies, still buzzing.

'Get me out of here!' said Finn. Feeling queasy, he raced for the door.

'Wait!' Snake warned, lunging at Finn, trying to stop him.

They both skidded out into the kitchen.

'Snake!' gasped Rosetta, as two sooty boys burst out of the pantry. Her hands were covered in soap bubbles. She was washing up dishes in the big stone sink.

Someone lounged at the table. It was Mr Bains, who'd just popped into the kitchen for a hot gin and water. He lumbered to his feet.

'Yes, Snake indeed! And what is you a-doing of, with your little pal? Is you running away from your dear old master? Butcher!' called Mr Bains. 'Runaways! Here is a job for you!'

At Mr Bains's command, a low growl came from under the kitchen table. A squashed pink nose appeared. Followed by a white head, smooth as a bullet, with a set of savage fangs. Then Mr Bains's bulldog, Butcher, came stalking out.

He was a champion rat-killing dog, feared all over town. He had stumpy bow legs and a great barrel chest. His face was scarred from many rat fights. He had one bulging, pink-rimmed eye – a rat had clawed out the other. His ears had been chewed off long ago. He wore a spiked silver collar, first prize in a rat-killing competition. No one, man or beast, messed with Butcher.

'Get 'em, boy!' yelled Mr Bains.

Butcher sprang at Finn and Snake. He seized Snake by his unmentionables and clung on fast. Meanwhile, Cook barred Finn's way, folding her brawny arms: 'You stay put, boy!'

'Good dog! Good dog!' laughed Mr Bains as Snake was shaken like a rat. Once Butcher got a grip, nothing would make him let go – only prising apart his jaws, or Mr Bains shouting, 'Drop it, boy!'

But Rosetta knew another way. Cook and Mr Bains had forgotten about her – she'd been invisible, as usual, but now she sprang into action. She snatched a big tin marked FLOUR from the shelf.

'Hey, put that down, girl!' shouted Cook.

Rosetta dashed up to Butcher. He was in a frenzy, foaming at the mouth, dragging Snake round the kitchen. She dumped the whole tin of flour on Butcher's head. A great white cloud covered the dog and her and her brother. Butcher was choking, his nose blocked, he had to open his mouth to breathe.

'Run!' yelled Rosetta. Snake ripped himself free, leaving a chunk of his unmentionables in Butcher's jaws.

Finn was on his toes too, ready to run, but not to warn Walter Closet. He planned to dash back to Superloo in the cellar and yell, 'Take me home! NOW!' He'd had quite enough of Victorian times.

But Cook had planted herself in front of the cellar door. Snake grabbed his sleeve. 'Come on!' Finn had no other choice. He ran, with Snake and Rosetta, out of the back door.

Butcher sneezed once, twice, to clear his nose. 'Drop it, boy!' said Mr Bains.

Butcher dropped the piece of Snake's trousers. Mr Bains gave it to him to sniff. 'Now find 'em, boy. Find 'em.' Butcher shot off through the back door.

'Good riddance!' said Cook. 'That slavey never knew her place. Far too uppity if you asks me.'

Upstairs, a bell was frantically jangling. Miss Gripper wanted more jelly. Another joined it. Lady Gripper wanted a fan picked up that was two steps from her sofa. But there was no one to answer the bells.

'Not my job,' said Cook. 'I ain't paid to climb all them stairs.'

Mr Bains sat down again, sipped his hot gin and water.

'I thought you would be off, Mr Bains,' said Cook, 'a-chasing them runaways.'

'No rush, ma'am,' said Mr Bains. 'I'm pretty sure where Snake and his sister is a-going. To Rats' Nest Yard, that stinking den of thieves they calls home. Butcher will track 'em down, easy. He'll keep 'em there till I come.'

Mr Bains was right. Fleeing from Gripper Towers, with Butcher not far behind, Snake abandoned all plans of trying to reach the railway station. Warning Walter Closet would have to wait. He and Rosetta ran, taking Finn with them to the one place they felt safe – Rats' Nest Yard.

'Master will tell the crushers!' panted Snake as they ran. The crushers often helped masters hunt down runaway apprentices.

'Crushers?' echoed Finn. They sounded scary.

'Crushers, peelers, cheese!' said Snake, shaking his head at Finn's ignorance.

'Cheese?' said Finn, even more puzzled.

Snake tried another word. 'Cops!'

'Oh, cops,' said Finn. Now he understood.

'Anyhow, even cops won't come into Rats' Nest Yard,' said Snake. 'If they knows what's good for 'em.'

As they ran, a thick yellow fog came swirling in from the river. It turned the sun into a pale, dirty disc and crept through the alleys and streets of the town. It was foul, evil-smelling stuff, but it seemed heaven-sent to Snake and Rosetta. Like a cloak of invisibility, it wrapped itself round the three children, hiding them from their pursuers.

It didn't stop Butcher, though. With his head down, snuffling at the cobbles, Mr Bains's champion rat-killing dog was still tracking them down. And going into Rats' Nest Yard after them didn't bother *him* one little bit.

CHAPTER SIX

While Finn, Rosetta and Snake were running to Rats' Nest Yard, down in the cellar of Gripper Towers, Superloo was having problems of its own. Its great escape wasn't going to plan.

'I bet Finn is at the railway station already!' it fretted. It should have been free by now, hovering to join him.

The coal heaps didn't delay it. It had hovered round some, over others, like a silver ghost in the darkness.

'*Wheee!*' the toilet was rejoicing, as it sailed up the ramp. 'This hover cushion is great! Nothing can stop me now!'

Then its sensors told it that the big trapdoor was bolted. It was bolted on the inside. That wouldn't have stopped a human for two minutes. But for Superloo, so brilliant in some ways, so helpless in others, it was a huge headache.

For a few seconds, the great toilet genius gave way to self-pity.

'Curse this ludicrous toilet body!' it wailed. 'Curse my lack of hands!'

If it had hands, it could have slid back the bolt in an instant. 'It just isn't fair!' it sobbed wildly. 'How can I, SUPERLOO, the greatest toilet of all time, be stopped by a stupid metal bolt?'

To comfort itself, it played its favourite tune, 'Drip, Drip, Drop Little April Showers'. The chirpy song echoed around the dismal coal heaps. It never failed to cheer Superloo up.

'Pull yourself together!' the great toilet genius scolded itself. 'Get a grip! Finn would be ashamed of you!'

Its computer brain began whirring. Surely it could solve this little difficulty? In precisely 2.5 seconds, it had.

'I shall use myself as a battering ram!' announced Superloo. 'I shall *smash* my way through that bolted door.'

To give itself maximum speed, it inflated the hover cushion even more. The airbag on its bottom bulged and wobbled like a living thing.

'Charge!' shrieked Superloo, powering up the ramp like a silver space rocket being launched.

Crash! The trapdoor shattered. The bolt bent, but still it held. Superloo's sensors assessed the damage.

'A couple more tries should do it!' crowed Superloo excitedly.

It hovered back to the bottom of the ramp to give itself a better run-up. At last it had found something its toilet body was perfect for. 'A human would be much too puny to do this,' it scoffed, having conveniently forgotten that a human being would just slide back the bolt.

Mr Bains had finished his hot gin and water. He was back in the stableyard, loading the last sacks of soot on to his donkey cart. Then he planned to trot his old donkey to Rats' Nest Yard to catch his runaway climbing boy. There was no hurry. Butcher would keep them cornered until he arrived. Besides, he'd already summoned the peelers and he was waiting for them to show up.

Then suddenly Mr Bains heard the most tremendous crash. He ran over to the trapdoor. 'What the devil is going on?' he asked himself, gazing at the smashed and splintered wood.

He knelt down to look closer.

Suddenly, from inside the cellar, he heard a strange tinny screech, 'Go for it, SUPERLOO! This one will do it!'

The trapdoor was hit from inside with shattering force. It buckled, and burst open.

'What the devil –?' began Mr Bains again.

His face barely had time to show terror. A huge metal box came hurtling up from the cellar. It almost mowed him down – he had to jump for his life!

'*Whoops!* Frightfully sorry!' came a muffled cry from inside the box.

Then it shot out of the stableyard. A triumphant shout trailed behind it: 'I'm free!'

Mr Bains lay sprawled where he'd landed, in the horse muck of the stableyard. He shook his head, bewildered. He didn't think he was *that* drunk. He staggered groggily to his feet.

'What *were* that flying silver thing?' he gasped.

Meanwhile, Superloo was whizzing through the gardens of Gripper Towers. Now it had escaped from the cellar, finding the railway station should be no problem. The great toilet genius had old maps of the town in its databanks. And its sensors were better than eyes, constantly feeding it details about its surroundings.

But something was wrong.

'Help!' yelled Superloo as it skittered through Lord Gripper's gardens, knocking the arms off all his very expensive marble statues.

It was having trouble controlling itself. For a start, its airbag seemed to be punctured – maybe a splinter of wood had stabbed it. Superloo sounded like Mr Brush's faithful hound, Blaster – leaking air from its bottom with loud *parping* sounds. And crashing into those trapdoors seemed to have temporarily scrambled some of its circuits. The toilet couldn't navigate; its sense of direction was totally shot.

'*Aaargh!*' shrieked Superloo, as it ploughed through a hedge, demolished a summer house and nearly fell into a lily pond.

The smog was still rolling in from the river. It had even reached the massive iron gates of Gripper Towers. It paused there a moment, as if it didn't dare enter, but then it began creeping into the gardens.

A carriage was driving away from the grand front entrance of the house. Lady Gripper and her brats were inside it. Even posher than their everyday carriage, it was in white and gold, drawn by four white horses. At the back stood two tall footmen in splendid uniforms, stockings and buckled shoes. They almost looked more toffee-nosed than the Grippers.

The carriage rolled down the drive. The Grippers were hours too early for the Queen's arrival, but Lady Gripper wanted to drive around the town to impress the common folk.

'We shall be the envy of all who see us,' she gloated.

'*Pooh*, Ma,' said Master Gripper. 'There is nothing but poor people down there and they don't matter. And, besides, we must beware gawotters. Those nasty men pwey on wich folk like us.'

Everyone rich was scared of garotters. They were the latest bogeymen. They crept up behind you and strangled you with a scarf, while their partner stole your wallet. Even peelers wore special leather anti-garotting collars, so they couldn't be choked.

'You booby,' sneered his sister. 'They wouldn't dare garotte a *Gripper*. Pa would have their guts for garters.'

Back in the garden, Superloo careered about,

leaving a trail of destruction behind it. But now the alarm was being raised. A gardener saw a large dark shape floating in the fog.

'*Oi*, you there!' he yelled, waving his rake.

Armed with rakes and hoes, other gardeners and gardeners' boys came running, and soon they were chasing Superloo down the main drive.

'Help!' shrieked Superloo as it hurtled through the fog, knocking down statues like skittles, and all the time, with rude tooting sounds, the air was hissing out of its hover cushion.

The Gripper coach was just turning out of the main gates as the out-of-control toilet caught up with it. As it rushed past, its airbag blasted out an especially loud, juicy raspberry.

'Oh my!' screeched Lady Gripper, covering her ears. 'What was that frightful sound? It is a sound no respectable lady should hear!' And she fell back, fainting among the cushions.

Suddenly the coach was surrounded by peelers. They'd come about the runaway climbing boy. But this, it seemed, was a far greater emergency.

A sergeant, in his tall top hat and

anti-garotting collar, poked his head into the coach.

Lady Gripper roused a little. 'An outrage, Sergeant, an outrage!' she moaned. Then fainted again.

'Did anyone get a glimpse of the villain?' asked the sergeant.

'Yes!' cried Master Gripper. 'I saw him through the fog. He was huge, a monster!' He raved on, his voice getting shriller. 'He is one of these nasty gawotting fellows, come to stwangle us!'

'And he trumped,' said the down-to-earth Miss Gripper. 'And made our ma faint.'

'And he have wrecked Lord Gripper's gardens too,' said the head gardener, almost in tears. 'Smashed his precious statues all to pieces!'

'Calm yourself, young sir,' the sergeant told the hysterical Master Gripper. 'We shall catch this trumping, garden-wrecking garotter, never fear.'

And the peelers pounded off into the fog, waving their truncheons, followed by the angry mob of gardeners waving rakes and the footmen from the Gripper coach, mincing behind, trying to stop their shiny buckled shoes from getting muddy.

Superloo knew it was being chased. Its

scrambled sensors told it that much. But it was helpless to escape its pursuers.

'That way!' bellowed a constable, pointing his truncheon as another muffled *terrrump*! sounded through the fog. 'The trumping garotter is going towards the town!'

'You've got it wrong,' Superloo was squawking as it flew, parping, down the hill. 'I am *not* a garotter. I have never broken the law in my life! I am a perfectly respectable toilet!' But with the clattering of policemen's boots and the shouts of the rake-waving gardeners, nobody heard it.

The airbag gave a final *psssssst*! It was totally deflated now. Superloo was a hoverloo no longer. It should have shuddered to a stop. But it didn't. The road down to town was as steep as a ski slope, so it went even faster.

'Mind out the way!' shrieked Superloo, as it streaked down the hill.

It was a good job the fog had kept folk indoors or more than one person would have met a sticky end, squashed flat as a pancake by a flying toilet.

Superloo skidded round a corner. 'Oh no!' it screeched. Its super-sharp E-nose had picked up pongs – dead dogs, sewage.

It knew what lay ahead. 'The river!' it quacked as it sailed down the bank and splashed into the green, scummy water. For a few seconds, the silver cubicle floated. Then, with a glug, it was sucked down into the murky depths.

Disappointed, the peelers stood on the bank. The sergeant had his handcuffs out to make an arrest. He put them away again.

'I fear we have lost our man, lads,' he said as they gazed down into the stinking water. A few bubbles plopped to the surface. Then even they stopped.

CHAPTER SEVEN

'**M**ind the booby trap!' warned Snake.

'*Whoa!*' Finn had been clattering after Snake and Rosetta, down a dark flight of steps. He stopped just in time, teetering on the last step. Below him was a pit. A terrible stench rose from it. He could see green oozy stuff in the bottom.

'What's down there?' gasped Finn, holding his nose. Then he said, 'Don't tell me. I don't want to know.'

Carefully, he stepped round the pit.

Rats' Nest Yard was four big houses, built round a courtyard. They had been grand houses once. But now they were slum dwellings, rented out by the room and packed with poor folk. Dodgy characters lived here too: coiners, forging money; criminals hiding out from the law. There were booby traps all over the place to keep out peelers and other unwanted visitors. Also escape routes, bolt-holes and secret passages that only the people who lived here knew about.

'We calls 'em rat runs,' said Snake.

They were crawling along one of those rat runs now, a slimy tunnel barely wide enough for a man to squeeze through. Finn fought against panic.

'Where are we going?' he begged. This reminded him too much of being stuck in that chimney.

Snake and Rosetta, ahead of him, didn't hear. They were taking Finn deep into Rats' Nest Yard, where even Butcher would have trouble finding them. Butcher seemed to have stopped chasing them, but Snake knew that the champion rat killer hadn't given up. He was waiting outside for his master, Mr Bains. And they would come in together.

'Mind yer 'ead!' called Rosetta, over her shoulder.

'Ow!' said Finn as he bashed his head on something. He looked up, got a glimpse of iron spikes and dived forward, just in time. An iron-spiked grid came thudding down, closing off the tunnel behind them. Another booby trap.

'I forgot about that one!' called Snake's muffled voice from the front.

Then suddenly the rat run ended. They all spilt out of the tunnel, into a larger space.

Thank goodness for that, thought Finn. But where were they? Some kind of dark room?

He staggered to his feet and looked down in disgust at his clothes. He was covered in soot and what looked like mud but probably wasn't. He smelt terrible.

Then Finn noticed they weren't alone. There was a rustling all around him. Heaps of rags on the floor stirred, began standing up, shuffling about.

Those are people! thought Finn.

Then, as his eyes became used to the gloom, he saw whole families, men, women and children, sleeping on rags and straw. Finn gazed around, shocked. He couldn't take them all in. But one tiny boy caught his attention.

He was skeleton-thin with a wizened little face, like a sick old man. And he was gnawing on a bit of potato peel. He stared at Finn with huge hungry eyes.

Finn fumbled desperately for his pocket. He

was sure he had some chocolate to give him. But he didn't have any chocolate, didn't even have a pocket. Those were in his twenty-first-century clothes.

Snake had come back to find him. 'Keep up. I thought we'd lost you!'

Finn stumbled after him, but he took one quick look over his shoulder. That little boy was still staring.

Now they were in the courtyard between the buildings. There were swarms of ragged, shoeless children and crying babies crawling about in the muck. Women fought and screeched at a water tap that was only turned on for an hour a day. Rising above the din, Finn heard beautiful birdsong. It made your heart ache to hear it. He looked up and saw a wild bird crammed into a tiny cage. It was a robin, singing for all it was worth.

People called out, ''Ello, Snake. Rosetta! 'Ow's yer pa today?'

'Still the same,' said Rosetta. And it was only then Finn remembered what Snake had told him, up on the rooftops of Gripper Towers, about his dad getting hurt in an accident.

Something slapped into Finn's face. He looked up.

At first he thought it was bats, hung upside down on a line. Then he smelt them. *Phew, fish*, he thought. They were herrings pegged out to dry. A woman in a bright red shawl snatched one down and pressed it into Rosetta's hand.

'There you are, deary,' she said. 'That's for yer poor pa. Toast it for 'im on the fire.'

Snake pulled down a hidden ladder from somewhere. And now they were climbing up out of the noisy, crowded courtyard.

Another rat run, a trapdoor, a passageway and then they were inside a room. As gloomy as the one before, but not so crammed with people. Finn could only see a few, huddled round a feeble fire.

A great four-poster bed took up half the room. It had belonged to the gentry who'd lived in these houses years ago. It was worm-eaten now and the curtains round it, once rich purple velvet, were faded and mouldy.

Rosetta pushed them aside. Finn saw a thin, feverish face on the pillow.

'How are you, Pa?' asked Rosetta. 'Mrs Rogers sent you a herring.'

Pa had risked his life to rescue a girl in Lord Gripper's factory. She'd been sent into the great oven before it had cooled down. It took forty-eight hours to cool down properly after the fires underneath had been put out, but Lord Gripper could never wait that long. 'I needs those pots NOW!' he'd thunder. 'It's a rush job!' So, after only twelve hours, workers were forced in to bring out the potties. The girl was the first. But when Snake's pa had heard her scream, 'I'm roasting!' he'd thrown wet rags over his face, dashed in and flung her out of the oven door. Before Pa could escape himself, he'd been badly burned.

Finn thought, *That poor guy looks ill. He shouldn't be in this awful place.*

He didn't know that Rosetta paid all her wages to rent Pa that bed. Normally, a whole family would sleep in it. Rosetta was wondering now how they were going to tell Pa that she and Snake were runaways. How could the family live without their wages? There'd be nothing for them but the Workhouse. Rosetta shuddered at the thought. It was the nightmare of all poor people, to be sent to the Workhouse.

No, she couldn't worry Pa with all that. Instead she said, 'Where's Lizzie?'

A girl, about five years old, came staggering

in. She looked spindly and frail, as if a puff of wind might blow her over. She was lugging a battered metal bucket. Water slopped over the sides. She'd been queuing at the tap, waiting her turn.

Lizzie was Snake and Rosetta's little sister. It was her job to stay at home and look after Pa.

Snake introduced Finn to Pa: 'This is my chimbley-climbing pal.'

Like Rosetta, he didn't want to worry Pa. He didn't mention that Butcher and Mr Bains were hunting them down. Instead, he told Pa, 'We're all a-going to warn Walter Closet.'

Quickly, he told Pa the rest, about Lord Gripper's evil potty plot that would get Walter Closet thrown in jail.

'And there ain't much time, Pa,' Snake finished up. 'Queen Vic's arriving at three o'clock.'

The sick man raised himself painfully off the pillow. 'That Lord Gripper,' he raved, 'he's the very devil! You must stop him, son!'

'Don't fret, Pa,' soothed Snake, seeing how worked up Pa was getting. 'We shan't let him ruin another good man.'

Finn had wandered over to the window. Snake and Rosetta were trying to make Pa comfortable, giving him sips of water, while Lizzie trotted over to the fire to toast the herring. People crowded round the fire moved aside and made room for her. In Rats' Nest Yard, her pa was known as a hero.

Pa's only thanks from Lord Gripper had been the sack and a whopping fine for holding up potty production.

Finn rubbed a spyhole in the grime and peered out. His heart thudded. He said, 'Mr Bains is here!'

Snake came rushing over. He saw Mr Bains clopping up on his donkey cart. Mr Bains gave it to a ragged lad to guard.

Butcher came swaggering over. He growled at the building, showing his yellow fangs.

'Patience, boy, patience,' said Mr Bains. 'You shall have 'em, soon enough.'

Then, with Butcher sniffing the ground ahead of him, Mr Bains strode into the building.

'They're coming in,' Snake told his sister in a grim voice.

'We must go, Pa,' said Rosetta. 'We must go to warn Walter Closet.'

And Snake whispered to the crowd round the fire, 'If Mr Bains comes in 'ere, swear you ain't seen us.'

They nodded. He knew they wouldn't betray him. People in Rats' Nest Yard didn't rat on each other.

The three hurried off, diving again into the rat runs. Snake was taking them out of the building another way.

But Mr Bains, with Butcher to guide him, was catching up. It had been a bad day so far. He'd lost his best climbing boy. Then he'd been almost squished by some strange metal contraption that could talk. When he'd told the peelers, they laughed themselves silly.

'Mr Bains,' they'd said. 'You must be drunk as a lord!'

But things were looking up. Soon he'd have that boy in his grasp. Then he'd chain him up every night, to make sure he didn't escape again.

'Butcher!' he yelled. Where was that blessed dog? This flight of stairs was very dark. 'Butcher, you varmint!' he called, shaking his fist.

Mr Bains went clumping down the stairs.

Suddenly there was a loud scream: 'Aaaaargh!'

Followed by a *plop*. Mr Bains had fallen into the cesspit booby trap that Finn had only just avoided.

Mr Bains surfaced from the gunge. Rats' Nest Yard was full of revolting smells, but this one beat the lot. Mr Bains's hair was plastered down with slime. He was waist-deep in something very nasty. The sides of the pit were too high for him to climb out. He did some spectacular cursing.

Then he yelled, 'Help! Is anybody there?'

Something jabbed into Mr Bains. It was a spiked collar.

'Butcher!' he cried, peering into the dim light of the pit.

The battle-scarred dog was paddling around happily. There was only one thing Butcher liked better than tracking down runaways. And that was killing rats.

As soon as he'd smelt them and seen their little red eyes glinting in the gloom, he'd deliberately dived in.

Snap! There went his savage jaws at another rat. *Snap!* There were hundreds down here. Butcher was in heaven!

Mr Bains was beginning to panic. A rat swam by, doing doggy-paddle. He felt whiskers brushing his face. Was that a rat nibbling his ear?

'Help!' he shrieked. 'Can any of you ragged wretches hear? I'll get the peelers on to you! I'll get you put in the Work'ouse! The whole dratted lot of you!'

Rats' Nest Yard was seething with people. It seemed impossible that no one heard Mr Bains, but not a single person came rushing to help.

Finn, Rosetta and Snake came sliding out of a secret gap between two buildings just at the place where Mr Bains had parked his donkey cart.

Snake said a few words to the boy holding the donkey's reins. Obligingly, the boy handed them over and vanished into the rat runs.

'Hop in!' cried Snake. 'Now we can ride to the station in style!'

'Wait,' said Finn.

He didn't know why he did it – it was a reckless and foolish thing. But he dashed back into the courtyard, dodged through the ragged crowds and opened the door of that robin's cage.

'Go on,' hissed Finn, waving his hands frantically, 'you're free!'

The robin stood for a moment in the open door, as if it couldn't believe it. Then it went shooting off into the sky.

Someone tried to grab him. 'Oi, you varmint! That's my bird, I trapped it!'

Finn twisted free and raced back outside.

'Right,' he said. 'Let's go.'

Snake gave the reins a flick and the old donkey started forward. With Rosetta and Snake up on the front seat and Finn sitting behind on the sacks of soot, they went trotting through the town.

The fog had cleared. Now the streets were packed and noisy.

'Buy my fine muffins!' someone bawled in Finn's ear. The iron-rimmed wheels of wagons on cobbles made a deafening clatter.

As the nippy little donkey cart cut through the throng, Finn glimpsed a barefooted girl selling watercress. Hot, greasy fumes wafted from a boiled-beef shop. Brightly coloured flags fluttered everywhere.

It was a big day for the little town. Everyone was dressed in their best, in holiday mood. Only Lord Gripper's workers hadn't been given time off to welcome the Queen. They were still slaving away in the potty factory.

Snake pointed it out as they drove past: 'That is Lord Gripper's factory.'

Finn saw a ramshackle collection of buildings and smoking chimneys with Big Bertha in the middle, towering over them all.

It was so bewildering. Finn felt like a stranger in his own hometown.

I don't even know where we are, he thought.

Then suddenly he spotted a familiar landmark. 'There's our town hall!'

But even that looked strange. It was brand spanking new, as if it had just been built. Its bricks were bright red, its columns snowy white. And, before it, was the statue of poor dead Prince Albert, looking heroic on a prancing horse. That looked new too – the bronze gleamed like fire.

We're in the town square, thought Finn, pleased that at last he'd got his bearings. *And the railway station should be just here.*

'*Whoa!*' said Snake, pulling the donkey up in front of it.

Right, thought Finn, sliding off the soot sacks, *let's get this over with.*

It should be straightforward. Warn Walter Closet, then back to Superloo in the cellar, then home.

And what about the 1812 Overture Toilet?

'Forget it,' Finn decided. Even if he saw it, was he really supposed to steal it? Somehow get it back to Superloo?

'Get real!' Finn told himself sternly. 'There's no chance. Just concentrate on getting *yourself* back.'

Down at the bottom of the river, a red light flashed through the murk. It said CLEANING.

As it sank, the great toilet genius had locked its cubicle door. Now it was watertight, but some smelly water had swilled inside and made pools on its gleaming floor so it was having a quick run through its cleaning cycle. As a final touch, it sprayed itself with Woodland Glade air freshener.

That's better, thought Superloo. It was time now to consider its options. Its circuits began to fizz.

But even its brilliant brain had to admit it. Things were looking rather bleak. Its airbag was punctured. If that had been functioning, it could have floated to the surface, but, without it, it was well and truly stuck – a twenty-first-century Superloo at the bottom of a Victorian river.

'There must be some way out,' quacked Superloo. But its usually bouncy voice was subdued.

Its storage batteries wouldn't last forever. In a few hours its cubicle lights would fail. Then its sensors, which kept it in touch with the outside world. And, finally, its brain would shut down completely.

Could it time travel back from the riverbed? It hated to abandon Finn, but it might have to, to save its own life. It tried setting time-travel coordinates. It didn't work. For some reason, it just couldn't take off underwater.

'I seem to be in a bit of a jam,' Superloo finally admitted.

Great black eels writhed around it. Water snails slithered over the airbag, gluing them-selves on with slime. Like a wrecked ship, Superloo was already being colonized by river creatures. Soon it would be completely covered by snails and waving weed. It would become part of the riverbed. And no one would know it was the last resting place of a great toilet genius.

'Oh dear,' sobbed Superloo, feeling very sorry for itself.

It turned off its cubicle lights to save power.

And out of the darkness came a chirpy but somehow strangely wistful little ditty. It was Superloo's comfort song: 'Drip, Drip, Drop Little April Showers'.

CHAPTER EIGHT

In the twenty-first century, Mr Lew Brush was in the town square too. But it looked very different to Victorian times. The town hall was shabby and neglected. Its white columns were grubby, its bricks black and crumbling.

'Smile!' shouted a man with a camera from the local paper. 'Hold up your banner!'

'Tell us what you think about the council!' yelled a TV news reporter, holding up a mike. 'We are live, on air!'

'I think they are a load of . . .' began Mr Brush. He then said some extremely rude words, which would have shocked daytime telly viewers. But, luckily, the clattering wings of pigeons in the town square drowned them out. And, besides, he was too far away from the mike. He was up on the statue of poor dead

Albert, seated behind the prince on the prancing bronze horse. He was clinging on for dear life.

The statue wasn't gleaming now. It was streaked with pigeon poo and green with age. These days, hardly anyone looked twice at it. The name of the guy on the horse had been forgotten. But now Mr Brush had joined him, it seemed the whole town knew who he was.

'Here up on the statue of Prince Albert,' the TV reporter was telling her viewers, 'Mr Brush is conducting a one-man campaign. He says he will not come down until the council promises not to sell the allotments.'

Up on the horse, Mr Brush was asking himself, 'What are you doing up here, you silly old fool? You must be crazy! You're far too old for all this!'

He wanted publicity, yes. But everything had got a bit out of hand.

When he'd come into the town square this morning – a little guy in green wellie boots and a duffle coat, carrying a big banner – no one had even seen him. He might have been invisible. He'd been barged aside by people in a hurry, his cries of 'Save our allotments!' lost in snarling traffic.

So he'd climbed up on to the statue. That had made people take notice.

He'd got out all his medals, won when he was parachuted behind enemy lines in World War II, and pinned them in rows on his duffle coat. They made a very impressive display.

'I'm an old soldier!' he'd yelled down to some curious onlookers. 'I fought for this country! And now I can't even grow my spuds in peace!'

That little crowd had swelled to a big one, cheering him on. Now there were TV cameras, reporters, police keeping back the people and an ambulance in case he fell off.

'*Whoops!*' Mr Brush felt himself slipping. He wrapped an arm round the prince's waist. Albert stared into the distance, looking hand-some and heroic.

'You'd have understood, wouldn't you, Albert?' whispered Mr Lew Brush into his cold bronze ear. Albert was dead keen on gardening – all the royal children had little plots where they grew their own vegetables.

Mr Brush shook his head sadly. That proved he really was crazy – talking to a statue.

He wished he'd never climbed up here, attracting so much attention.

'I wonder if Blaster has woken up yet?' he worried. He'd left the ancient hound back on the allotment, tucked up and snoozing in his basket, convinced that the cabbage-headed dummy was really his dear old master.

And there was another thing. It had been nagging away at Mr Brush for ages, as he sat up on the horse. Suddenly it exploded in his mind, like a dazzling light.

'Wheelie-bin collection day is Tuesday!'

So what had that green crusher van been doing today, Saturday, snooping about by the allotments emptying bins? Bin men don't even work on a Saturday.

All sorts of awful suspicions came flooding into Mr Lew Brush's mind.

'You silly old fool!' he scolded himself. There was definitely something dodgy going on. He should have realized right away. But, instead, he was sitting up here playing the big star, with cameras snapping all around him.

Mr Brush let go of Albert. He left his banner behind, draped over the horse's bronze bottom, and began to slide off the statue.

People rushed forward to help him, shouting questions, but Mr Lew Brush ignored them. None of the crowd of supporters existed for him now, or the reporters or TV cameras. All he was thinking was, *Superloo may be in danger*.

He was really furious with himself. He should have been protecting his friend Superloo. But he'd let his guard down. And, worse than that, he'd made himself into a celebrity. Now everyone wanted to know his business.

As he tried to force his way through the crowd, people were sticking mikes and cameras into his face.

'Mr Brush, have you anything to say?'

They just wouldn't let him alone. They'd want to know where the allotments were next. And Mr Brush knew that, if they followed him back there, they'd surely find out about Superloo. How the world's press would love that! A public convenience that can talk, that has a super-intelligent brain. They'd be camping out on his doorstep – Superloo's picture would be splashed all over the papers. The great toilet genius would be treated like some kind of freak.

'Have you anything to say to our viewers?'

yakked the lady reporter again. 'Mr Brush? Mr Brush? Where are you going?' She ran after him.

Mr Brush desperately tried to think. Where could he hide? He gazed around. Then, bingo, he had the answer.

'Mr Brush, have you given up your campaign?'

'No way,' said Mr Brush, shuffling in his wellies towards a low concrete building.

'So where are you going?' she shrilled, shoving a mike into his face again.

Mr Brush didn't want to be rude – there were ladies present. 'I have just come down from the horse to pluck a rose,' he said.

And, with great dignity, he entered a door marked GENTS.

For a brief moment, there was peace and quiet. He was alone in the toilets. He looked around frantically. There was an open window at the back. Where did it lead to? His old bones creaked as he climbed up on the sink and thrust his head through.

Good. There was an alleyway out the back. It was overflowing with rubbish bins but there was no sign of any people.

He turned round precariously on the sink

and squeezed wellies first through the window, using a bin as a stepping stone. Then he was down in the alley. He hadn't known his old body was so nimble – but you can do anything if you're desperate enough.

'What now?' he asked himself. He had to get away from here, fast. They'd soon come swarming into the toilets and find him gone.

It was no good waiting for a bus. They didn't come for hours and then three came at once. He would just have to resort to other tactics. In the war, he'd got himself out of situations much stickier than this.

Mr Brush crept down the alley. And there was the answer to his prayers. Rows and rows of bicycles, left by their owners. Mr Brush quickly checked the ranks. There would be at least one that wasn't locked – there always was. It was a beat-up old lady's bike with a basket on the front. Checking around to see that no one was watching, Mr Brush climbed on and began to pedal.

The bike's owner wasn't going to be pleased. *But I'm only borrowing it*, thought Mr Brush. *This is an emergency*.

He cycled away towards the allotments as fast as his creaky old legs would turn. His face was grim. He was almost certain that Super-loo's enemies had, once again, tracked it down. The question was: what sinister and scary toilet terminators had they sent this time?

Back at the allotment, while Blaster dozed in Mr Brush's shed, there was movement down by the gate. Two men climbed out of the plastic wheelie bins. They were swathed from head to foot in black – only their gleaming eyes showed. They were ninja assassins, expert in all martial arts. Their hands alone were lethal weapons, but hidden beneath their robes they had daggers and throwing stars as backup.

Their ninja names were Wildcat and Cobra. And they could strike just as fast and silently as those deadly killers.

In a graceful curve, one backflipped over the allotment fence. Like his wildcat namesake, he didn't make a sound as he landed. With a stunning leap, Cobra soared after him, twirling twice in mid-air.

Stealthily, they crept towards the allotment sheds. They'd been told the toilet they sought was in one of them. But which? Their eyes were cold and glittering. They showed no fear at all. No one escaped the ninja assassins.

Suddenly there was more movement down by the gate. The lid of an old metal dustbin was pushed off. It made a dreadful clanging racket as it rolled.

Another ninja climbed out, smaller than the others.

Wildcat and Cobra glanced at each other. They didn't say a word – total silence when working was the ninja code – but Cobra raised one eyebrow as if to say, 'Typical!' Trust their ninja companion to choose a noisy metal bin to hide in.

The third ninja attempted a springy leap over the allotment fence. He landed with a crash among the vegetables.

This time Wildcat did break the code. He sighed. Then put a finger to his head and screwed it round as if to say, '*Doh!* What an idiot.'

They usually worked together, just the two of them, a lethal and efficient team. But this time they'd been forced to bring a ninja apprentice along. They couldn't refuse; he was a nephew of the grand master. But the young apprentice was the most useless ninja ever. His ninja name was Dung Beetle, because he was as bumbling and clumsy as that insect.

Dung Beetle crawled to his knees and crouched among the cabbages and peas. He peered over them. His eyes weren't those of a cold-blooded killer. They were creased up with worry.

Cobra jerked a thumb towards Mr Brush's shed. The message was clear: you search that one. Dung Beetle rushed to obey, only once sprawling to the ground after getting a pea stick stuck up his baggy trousers.

He should have made a dazzling leap up to the roof, then run lightly along the top. That's what proper ninjas do. But Dung Beetle wasn't too good at acrobatics, so he just walked up and opened the door. He forgot the ninja code and gave a loud '*Hai!*' of surprise.

He could hardly see in the gloomy shed, but he'd made out a shape. There was someone in here! Sitting in that chair, with a floppy hat pulled down low on his head.

In a panic, Dung Beetle struck out, chopping with the edge of his hand at the guy's neck, as he'd been taught at ninja school.

Then '*Hai!*' he cried again, in even greater surprise, as the man's head, still with the hat on, fell off and rolled slowly across the floor.

Dung Beetle stood dazed, staring at his own hand. Did it really do that? And he'd always been bottom of the class at karate!

The head came to a stop by Blaster's basket. Blaster woke up. The old hound blinked half-blind eyes. What was that? He took a sniff at the fishing hat. It smelt of Mr Brush. But what had happened to his dear old master? Had he fallen to pieces? Blaster raised his baggy head and saw Dung Beetle standing there, still stunned with amazement at his own powers.

Did the old hound crumple into a hopeless, tooting heap? Did he lift up his head and howl dismally? He did not. For once Blaster astonished himself. He found strength he didn't know he had. He became Superdog!

With savage fury, he hurled himself at Dung Beetle, his few wobbly old teeth glinting like fangs, his mouth foaming.

Dung Beetle saw the furry fiend hurtling towards him. Its eyes flashed like a hound from hell. Like all ninjas, Dung Beetle was deeply superstitious.

'A spirit dog!' he gibbered. With glowing eyes, as big as truck headlights!

He didn't even have time to get out his throwing star. In any case, he'd forgotten it. And, besides that, everyone knows that spirit dogs can't be killed. His black trousers flapping, he dashed out of the door.

The heroic hound collapsed in a heap. He'd exhausted himself.

Outside, the fleeing Dung Beetle found Cobra and Wildcat. They'd found nothing in the sheds they'd searched. Remembering the ninja code of silence, Dung Beetle did a frantic mime, his hands chopping wildly. Now he seemed to be trying to pull off his own head.

Cobra looked at Wildcat. His brows scrunched up, as if to say, 'What's that loony boy on about now?'

Cobra glanced through the door of Mr Brush's shed. Even he let out a surprised '*Hai!*' He beckoned Wildcat over. They both stared in. They didn't see Blaster, who'd crawled under the table. All they saw was the headless dummy, which didn't look like a dummy in the dark.

Dung Beetle nodded and pointed to himself as if to say, 'I did that. With my bare hands.'

The heads of Cobra and Wildcat shook slowly in dumb amazement.

Then they heard a grinding at the allotment gate. It was the bin van coming back to pick them up.

Cobra and Wildcat twirled and backflipped towards it while Dung Beetle lumbered behind. The two ninja assassins hadn't found the toilet yet but they'd certainly found something out about Dung Beetle. As the bin lorry drove off, with all three of them crammed inside, they looked at the apprentice ninja with new respect.

'Your uncle, the grand master, will be very pleased when he hears of this,' said Cobra.

Wildcat nodded in solemn agreement. 'Hai.'

And Dung Beetle, even though he didn't know how on earth he'd done it, glowed with pride.

Mr Brush, pedalling the battered old bike like a maniac, arrived back just as the bin van was pulling away. He threw the bike into his potato patch. When he saw his shed door was ajar, he knew something was wrong.

He rushed in. 'Blaster!' he yelled. 'Are you all right?'

Happy yelps came from under the table.

Blaster came wheezing towards his master and slobbered all over him in pure joy.

Mr Brush threw his arms round his faithful hound. 'Thank goodness you're safe, my dear old friend!'

Mr Brush looked round the shed. He saw the dummy had been disturbed. 'What's been going on here?' he said. It was obvious someone had been inside. 'Were they searching for Superloo?' he asked Blaster.

What's the good of asking Blaster? thought Mr Brush. The poor old dog had probably been trembling in his hiding place during the search.

'Never mind, my old mate,' said Mr Brush, stroking Blaster's scabby nose. 'I'm back now. Don't be scared.'

Blaster's tail thumped feebly on the floor. He was ecstatic to see Mr Brush safe and in one piece. That was all that mattered to him.

What a shame, though, that Mr Brush would never know how noble and brave his old hound had been.

The toilet hunters seemed to have gone, but Mr Brush's eyes became flinty. He must keep on the alert. He must never let his guard down again.

'They'll be back,' he told Blaster. One thing was for sure: 'We're not safe here any more,' said Mr Brush. When Superloo returned, they would have to find somewhere else for the great toilet genius to hide.

CHAPTER NINE

Finn, Snake and Rosetta had tied up their donkey cart outside the railway station, then sneaked inside.

Finn stared around. A majestic glass-and-iron roof soared above them, sheltering the trains and platforms.

Finn couldn't remember that in the twenty-first century and he'd been to the station quite a few times.

Maybe I just never looked up, he thought.

The station was vast and empty and echoing as a cathedral. No iron monsters came clanking in. They'd all been cancelled to make way for the royal train. And the common people had been banished outside, into the town square. Only VIPs like the Grippers could meet the Queen. And even they might only get a glimpse. A ceremony had been planned to present the 1812 Overture Toilet, with people waving flags and cheering, and a silver band playing 'God Save the Queen'. But who knew what the Queen would do? She wasn't the world's most cheerful monarch. If she was feeling gloomy, she wouldn't even step off the train. She'd just stare stony-faced out of the window and steam off to Scotland.

'There be Walter Closet,' said Rosetta.

She pointed further up the platform where a group of people crowded round what seemed to be a wardrobe.

'Which one is Walter?' hissed Finn.

'The only one who ain't wearing a hat,' said Snake.

Then, among the posh top hats and bonnets, Finn saw an explosion of yellow straw-like hair. It belonged to a lanky young man with goggly eyes, green as gooseberries, and egg stains on his waistcoat. The wardrobe, with the 1812 Overture Toilet inside, had just been moved out of the luggage office, ready for the Queen's arrival. And now Walter Closet was about to explain his invention to a group of VIPs.

'Ladies and gentlemen,' he said, waving his arms wildly about. 'May I introduce you to the world's most advanced toilet!'

He threw open the wardrobe doors.

The wardrobe was a massive, forbidding piece of furniture, like a giant oak coffin, with spiky crowns on top.

Finn craned forward to get a glimpse of Superloo's famous relative, but curious onlookers hid it from view.

'We must get closer,' whispered Snake, 'and speak to Walter.'

'*Oi!*' Finn felt a hand on his collar.

It was a policeman, in his hard top hat, with a truncheon and handcuffs clinking on his belt. The peeler saw two soot-covered climbing boys and a little slavey, in her mob cap and coarse apron.

'This isn't the place for the likes of you!' boomed the peeler. 'Be off! Only gentry is allowed!'

His loud voice echoed along the platform. The toffs around the wardrobe turned and stared. Walter Closet summed up the situation immediately.

'Let them stay, Constable,' he said. 'Let them see my toilet.'

He beckoned them closer. Was it because he'd once been just a common gardener's boy? 'Any one of these children could become a famous inventor,' he said.

The constable barked, 'Go on, you 'eard Mr Closet! Look sharp now!' And he pushed them forward to join the throng around the toilet.

Ladies wrinkled their noses in disgust and drew their skirts away. 'Such dirty ragged children,' one shuddered.

Nervously, Rosetta looked around for the Grippers.

But they hadn't arrived yet. Lord Gripper was still at his factory, supervising the evil potty plot, and Lady Gripper and her horrid brats were still parading around the town in their carriage.

Now they were up close, Finn saw Superloo's relative for the first time.

'Wow!' he breathed.

It was a splendid loo, truly fit for a queen. Just as Superloo had described, its toilet bowl was a noble, crouching lion; its seat the finest mahogany. Its chain and cistern were glittering gold.

But it was the advanced toilet technology that made it so amazing. As he talked about his invention, Walter Closet's froggy eyes bulged alarmingly. His arms whirled even faster, like windmills.

Finn recognized the signs. 'Another toilet

freak,' he murmured. Mr Lew Brush would have loved him. Superloo would have chatted to him for hours.

'Its flush is ten times more powerful than any of Thomas Crapper's toilets,' Walter Closet raved. 'I have connected it to a water tank, so I can demonstrate!'

And, carried away with enthusiasm, he snatched an ostrich-feather hat off a lady's head.

He dangled the hat over the toilet bowl. Its great curly plumes waved grandly in the air.

'My hat!' screamed the lady. 'How dare you!'

But Walter didn't seem to hear. He dropped it in and gave the gold chain a tug. There was a clanking from somewhere in the cistern. Then a sinister gurgling sound, then a *whooshing*. And suddenly a whirlpool raged in the toilet bowl. It swirled and, with one mighty gulp, it sucked the hat and its feathers out of sight.

There was applause from the watching toffs. 'Most impressive!'

But Walter Closet sighed. He wasn't satisfied yet. 'I wish,' he murmured, 'that I could make the flush more silent.'

Every Victorian toilet manufacturer was trying to crack that problem, but none of them had found the secret yet. What was the good of having music to cover your embarrassing sounds when the house-shaking flush told everyone, 'I've just been to the loo!'

'That hat cost me twenty guineas,' the lady was squawking.

'Never fear, ma'am!' cried Walter Closet. 'Your hat is quite safe!'

He dashed round the back of the toilet, where the water flowed through an outlet pipe into another tank. He fished around for a bit and scooped out a soggy mess.

He gave the hat a quick wring out and handed it back. The lady had no choice but to plonk it on her head. For, of course, it is the height of bad manners to meet the Queen hatless. The waving plumes that once stood so proud and tall flopped over her face and dripped toilet water down her neck.

She glared at Walter Closet as if she'd like to kill him, but the great toilet inventor didn't notice. He was too busy explaining about the music.

'Any embarrassing sounds,' he said, coughing discreetly, 'will be completely muffled by *The 1812 Overture*.'

Everyone murmured in admiration. They all knew that stirring warlike music, with its sounds of battle, including great cannon booms.

'I only have to press this lever, like so,' said Walter Closet, 'and the first notes of the overture will ring out!'

But he didn't do it. He was saving that for his next demonstration, which he hoped would be to Queen Victoria herself. And, anyway, the music must be stopped before flushing. It was most important to do that. The combined effect of the powerful flush and the cannon booms might be too much for the toilet mechanism.

He closed the wardrobe door. The demonstration was over. The VIPs scattered.

'I do hope,' Walter Closet whispered to himself, 'that the Queen gives my toilet her Royal Approval.'

If she did that, he knew he'd sell loads. Everyone would want a Walter Closet loo.

Walter Closet felt a tug at his sleeve. 'Beg pardon, sir,' said a tiny voice. Reluctantly, he dragged his mind away from his toilet dreams. His gooseberry eyes swivelled down.

'Sir,' Rosetta said. 'You must listen to me. You are in great danger.'

It took a long time for Finn, Rosetta and

Snake to get Walter Closet to take them seriously. It wasn't that he didn't believe them. It was just that his mind kept drifting away to lavatories. He reminded Finn of Superloo in some ways – a genius with a childish side who needed looking after.

'Sir,' said Snake desperately. 'We ain't got much time. The Queen arrives in two hours and we must stop Lord Gripper giving out these free chamber pots. I don't know why, but they will cause a riot. You will be locked up!'

'Yes,' Rosetta chimed in. 'You will be blamed. For it is *your* name that is on these pots.'

At last Walter Closet seemed to wake up to the dangers. '*My* name?' he gasped. 'On *chamber pots?*'

He was really shocked. His factory never made chamber pots. To him, they were as outdated as dinosaurs. He only made flush toilets, and those were of the most modern, revolutionary designs.

'We must rush to prevent this outrage!' he spluttered. 'My reputation in toilet circles will be ruined!'

This seemed to matter to him more than being banged up in jail and forced to grind bones for the rest of his life.

'We must hurry to Lord Gripper's factory!' he raved. 'Find these potties and destroy them!'

Meanwhile, down at the bottom of the river, Superloo thought, *Hey! Something's happening!*

It stopped playing 'Drip, Drip, Drop Little April Showers'. Like magic, its gloom and despondency lifted.

'I can inflate my airbag!' the great toilet genius crowed triumphantly.

But what had happened to that slow puncture? Very carefully, Superloo pumped up its hover cushion a bit more. No air leaked out.

Its brilliant brain gave it the answer. 'Saved – by water snails!' They'd glued themselves on, all over the hover cushion, in slimy clots, and some of them must have plugged up the hole.

'I can float to the surface now!' warbled Superloo.

It couldn't wait to rise from the murky depths. It was mad with impatience. There was so much to do! Find Finn, for a start, and its toilet relative.

'They *need* me up there!' wailed the great toilet genius. Humans had such inferior brain power. 'Without ME in charge,' fretted Superloo, 'they're probably making a right mess of things.'

And there wasn't much time to wrap this mission up. Soon, Superloo's storage batteries would run dangerously low.

But, for once, it didn't rush headlong into action. Because its brilliant brain told it, 'Take things slowly!' Too much air all at once might blast off the snails that were plugging the hole, and it would be stranded down here forever.

'Gently, gently,' the toilet warned itself, as it pumped in more air. It would just have to inflate the bag on its bottom a little bit at a time.

CHAPTER TEN

'**O**ur donkey cart is outside,' Snake told Walter Closet. 'We shall take you to Lord Gripper's potty works.'

Snake led the way and Rosetta, Finn and Walter followed.

But, privately, Snake was thinking, *I hopes we ain't too late.* What if Lord Gripper's hired thugs were already passing out potties amongst the crowd?

As the donkey cart left the station it met the Gripper coach lumbering in.

'Out of my way, wretch,' cried the coachman, leaning down and cutting at Snake with his whip. 'Do you not know whose carriage this is?'

Master Gripper's head poked out, with its angelic blond curls and screwed-up, spiteful face. He shook his tiny fist and shrilled, 'Yes, out of our way or I shall have you awwested!'

Rosetta hid her face, but there was no need. The Grippers were too full of their own importance to recognize their runaway slavey.

Snake trotted the old donkey through the crowded streets.

Everyone was in happy holiday mood, waving flags and shouting, 'God save the dear old Queen!' That meant they couldn't have seen the potties yet, because when they did, according to Lord Gripper, they'd become an angry mob in an instant, baying for Walter Closet's blood.

'Gee up!' said Snake, flicking the reins. Maybe they weren't too late, after all.

Now they were outside Lord Gripper's factory. From the front, the potty works was like a fortress. It was behind a spiked iron fence. After the workers came shuffling in at six in the morning, the great iron gates were locked. They didn't open again until nine at night when the workers were set free.

'I shall go inside!' declared Walter Closet. 'I shall confront Lord Gripper, man to man! Demand to know what he means by this – this potty fakery!'

He strode towards the gates. Under his egg-stained waistcoat, his skinny chest swelled. His green goggly eyes blazed with fighting spirit.

'No, sir, I beg you, do not!' said Rosetta, pulling him back. She knew what a monster the potty magnate was. It was like a butterfly taking on a warthog.

And already, from behind the gates, someone was eyeing them suspiciously. He was one of Lord Gripper's heavies, an ex-bare-knuckle fighter, with a broken nose and a bald head seamed with scars. It was his job to stop any strangers snooping around. Lord Gripper didn't want any busybodies, do-gooders or factory inspectors knowing how badly he treated his workers. How he employed little children. How he didn't give a fig about safety. How his workers were fined, even beaten, by brutal foremen for whistling or talking or trying to open a window to get some relief from the stifling heat.

Walter Closet tutted in disgust.

'This factory is a disgrace!' he fumed. 'It should have been demolished long ago! See that ancient chimney? I declare! How it does not fall down is beyond me!'

'Come away, sir' begged Rosetta.

The thug was unlocking the gate to challenge them. 'Oi, what's your game?' he was shouting.

Rosetta dragged Walter Closet back to the cart. Reluctantly, he climbed in.

'There must be another way in,' said Rosetta.

'There is,' said the resourceful Snake.

He trotted the little donkey down a stinking alley. On one side was the high wall of the potty factory. In it was a door.

'It's locked,' said Walter Closet.

'I knows that,' said Snake. '*That* is the way in.'

He pointed upwards to a window. It was tiny. But a chimney climbing boy could wriggle through any space.

'I climbs through there,' explained Snake. 'Then opens the door to let you in. Then we searches the place for these fake potties.'

'A most excellent plan!' said Walter Closet.

'Come on, Finn,' said Snake.

'Me?' said Finn, horrified. 'You want *me* to come with you?'

'Yer a chimbley climbing boy, ain't ya?' said Snake. ''Ere, I'll give you a leg-up!'

And soon Finn was clinging on to the wall

by the window. It was easier than he'd thought. The wall was crumbling too, like the rest of the factory. There were lots of gaps he could wedge his hands and feet in.

Finn thought, *I'm getting good at this*.

But suddenly his legs started shaking – because he'd just tried the window. He looked down dizzily to where Rosetta and Walter waited in the alley below.

'It won't open!' he called.

But Snake had shinned up beside him. 'You ain't afeerd, is ya?' he asked as Finn hung on for dear life by his fingers and toes. 'Why, this is nothing for a chimbley climbing lad!'

'I'm not a –' protested Finn. But there was no use going into all that now. He gabbled again, 'It's shut tight.'

'That don't matter,' said Snake. 'I don't do it no more, but I were a snakesman once. That's how I got my name.'

'A snakesman?' echoed Finn in a strangely shrill voice, trying hard not to look down.

''Pon my word, you is green!' said Snake, astonished. 'A snakesman is a kid what breaks into houses. He wiggles through tiny winders, like this one. Then lets his masters in, what are the *real* villains, to do the thieving –'

'I'm slipping,' gasped Finn through gritted teeth.

Snake didn't appear to have heard. 'Any'ow,' he continued casually, 'I were a bad lad.'

He shook his head sadly.

'I liked the roving life, see. I took off for London. I weren't no more than seven years old! At first I nearly starved. Then I got into ice thieving. That were a good scam. I chopped ice off ponds in rich folks' gardens. Sold it back to their own cooks, for to make ice-cream puddings! But I had to give that up – I had a bit of trouble. Then I got into *real* bad company and become a snake-sman. But when I heard about Pa's accident I come rushing back home –'

'Look,' interrupted Finn. 'Do you mind if we skip the life story?'

'Orl right,' said Snake, sounding hurt. He'd had a very colourful life for a fourteen-year-old.

'Look, it's not that I'm not interested,' Finn gabbled. 'It's just that I'm *going to fall*!'

'Oh, are ya?' said Snake. 'I didn't realize.'

And in one slick movement he put his elbow through the window glass, sneaked his hand in and lifted the catch. The window swung open.

'Git yerself in,' he said, shoving Finn head first through the tiny space.

'*Aaaargh!*' Finn landed with a bone-jarring thump on a pile of sacks. White clay dust rose in clouds. He started coughing.

'*Shhh!*' said Snake, landing soft as a cat on the ground beside him. 'We're in the drying room.'

A stove in the middle of the floor flared red and spat out sparks.

'It's roasting in here,' Finn panted.

All around them were shelves and shelves of potties, stacked right up to the ceiling. But they obviously weren't the fake potties. These were straight off the potter's wheel with the clay still wet. They were a long way from being finished. They had to be dried out and glazed, then fired in Big Bertha, the great bottle-shaped oven, then painted.

'Hide!' hissed Snake as the door shot open.

They ducked behind a potty stack. A small boy rushed in. There was a potty on his head, balanced on a board. The boy looked ready to drop from exhaustion, his little legs buckling. His feet were bare.

'A runner,' whispered Snake.

But he wasn't running fast enough. A voice bawled from outside, 'Faster, you idle varmint!' Someone had another potty ready to take to the drying room. Each potter had to make a hundred a day, so the runners could never rest.

The runner tottered away and Snake and Finn crept to the drying-room door. They peered out into a courtyard.

It was like a scene from hell. The great oven squatted like a monster in the middle, hissing and steaming.

'That's where Dad had his accident,' whispered Snake.

Around Big Bertha rushed ghostlike figures – potty workers covered in white dust. Sweat streaked their faces and stuck their hair to their scalps. Some struggled with wheelbarrows full of clay. Others carried strange clay boxes on their heads, staggering under the weight.

'What are those boxes they're carrying?' asked Finn.

'Saggars,' answered Snake. 'That's how the potties goes into the oven. They gets piled into saggars first, stops 'em from cracking.'

He stepped outside. Finn followed. 'We must take a peep in them saggars,' Snake whispered. 'See if the fake potties is inside.'

'And what be you two a-doing of?' growled a menacing voice.

'*Ow!*' said Finn. He felt a stick slash his legs. A great ham fist seized him. He looked up. A cruel face stared down. It was one of Lord Gripper's foremen, an ex-convict with a shaved head. His arms and chest swirled with sinister blue tattoos. He'd already grabbed Snake in his other hand.

'Let me go!' yelled Snake, kicking. But the foreman was too strong. He hauled them to the great oven. The fires underneath it were out, but it hadn't cooled down yet – its bricks were hot to the touch.

'Git in there!' ordered the foreman. 'Help unload them saggars.'

Potty workers came stumbling out of Big Bertha's door. Their hands and bare feet were wrapped in wet rags, to stop them getting burnt. They had caps on, but they could still feel the hot saggars scorching their heads. They lifted them off, their faces twisted with pain. A boy broke open the saggars, like cracking an egg, and lifted out the freshly fired potties.

'They're not the fake ones,' hissed Finn.

They were just bog-standard potties – plain, shiny and white, not shocking at all. And on the bottom was stamped not Walter Closet's name but GRIPPER'S SUPERIOR SANITARY PRODUCTS.

'I spy strangers!' someone growled. It was the guard from the gate. 'I seen them loitering outside. They're troublemakers, I'll warrant.'

'Fetch Lord Gripper,' ordered the foreman. 'And, till he comes, you can cool your heels in Big Bertha.'

And he shoved them into the great oven and bolted the door.

'Let me out of here!' yelled Finn. He hammered on the door, but even that was hot: it blistered his knuckles. The hot dust made him cough; he felt as if his eyeballs would fry. He smelt burning rubber – the oven floor was melting the soles of his boots.

The air scorched his lungs. 'I can't breathe!' gasped Finn.

And all the time Big Bertha cracked and groaned as she cooled down.

'This oven ain't safe!' said Snake grimly.

'Never mind that, I'm being barbecued!'

'I'll get us out.'

'How?' choked Finn. The door was bolted. Great towering piles of saggars surrounded them, so hot you could barely touch them.

'Up there!' said Snake. He was already climbing as nimbly as a squirrel up the saggar stacks. He climbed so fast he didn't even get scorched, like someone sprinting over burning coals.

Finn, squinting through hot, gritty eyes, watched him go. And now Snake was wobbling on the top saggar. Where would he go next? He sprang for the oven walls and, spread out like a starfish, he swarmed up them until he vanished up the chimney, the black hole right at the oven's centre.

Finn was weak and dizzy from the heat – he'd pass out any minute. He had a moment of pure panic. *What if he leaves me here?*

But Finn should have known better. The metal door to Big Bertha swung open. An arm reached in. 'Come on!' Snake yanked him out. All Finn wanted to do was collapse on the ground, gasping and flapping like a landed fish, but Snake made him run.

They would have been chased. Not by the zombie-like potty workers, but by Lord Gripper's hired thugs. Only something was happening behind them.

When Snake climbed up the saggars he'd made them rock. They'd swayed more wildly.

Then, domino-like, they all came clattering down. It was too much for Big Bertha. Her brickwork was already crumbling from years of heating and cooling. With a frightful wrenching sound, a great crack appeared in her side. It gaped wider, like an awful wound.

Despite the foreman's threats and curses, the potty slaves stopped working. They stood and stared. They couldn't believe it. Big Bertha was breaking up.

CHAPTER ELEVEN

In the alley, Rosetta and Walter Closet were still waiting with the donkey cart.

Walter Closet gazed at the locked door. What was going on in there? Why weren't Finn and Snake letting them into the potty factory?

Rosetta was worried too. 'They've been gone a long time.'

Then suddenly she grasped Walter Closet's arm.

'Look,' she whispered. Down at the alley's end the smelly river slid past, as thick and sludgy as porridge. A long black barge was coming into view. Lord Gripper's hired thugs came hurrying towards it, carrying piles of potties. A voice roared, 'Curse you! Load faster! The old bat will be here in an hour!'

''Tis Lord Gripper!' Rosetta trembled. She'd heard that savage bellow loads of times.

And he was obviously talking about the Queen.

Rosetta shrank back into the shadows. She could imagine his furious red face, his two wolf teeth glinting.

'Those must be the fake potties!' said Walter Closet.

They were loading them on to the barge and sailing them down to the railway station. It was only ten minutes away by river.

'We must stop them,' said Walter Closet. 'But how?'

His gooseberry eyes bulged in distress. His hands yanked at his mop of straw hair.

'What's up?' said a voice beside him.

'Snake, you're back!' said Rosetta, relieved. Snake and Finn were in an awful state, their ragged clothes scorched and smeared with soot and clay dust. But at least they were safe.

Walter Closet pointed to the end of the alley. 'I believe those are the potties we're looking for.'

With Rosetta leading Mr Bains's old, grey donkey, they crept to the end of the alley. Walter Closet peered out.

'We're helpless,' he said, wringing his hands in despair. Lord Gripper's thugs were out in force, some loading the barge, some keeping a lookout. Even the daredevil Snake had to agree. He shook his head grimly. 'It don't look good. They'll grab us, soon as we shows our faces.'

It seemed they were ready to go. The potties were loaded; Lord Gripper and his thugs were on board. The barge steamed away from the bank.

Walter Closet watched them go. His eyes were tragic. He still didn't know quite why, but those potties, once people saw them, would be his downfall.

His glittering career in toilets was finished. He bowed his head in despair.

Then Snake gripped his arm. 'Look!'

The barge was rocking! The potties and people on board were sliding about. Thugs were shouting out in alarm, as they shot across the deck. One hung over the side: 'There be a monster down there!' he cried. 'A great silver monster!'

'What's happening?' said Rosetta, bewildered.

The barge seemed to rise on a great fountain of spray. Potties and people were thrown out. Thugs were struggling in the water. Then a great gleaming cubicle rose majestically from the waves.

'What in heaven's name is *that*?' gasped Walter Closet.

Even Finn was amazed. What was Superloo doing in the river? He'd left the great toilet genius in the cellar of Gripper Towers.

But what did that matter? There was a grin a mile wide on Finn's face. 'Good old Superloo!' he cried.

You could always rely on Superloo. Well, to be strictly honest, you couldn't. But, this time, the great toilet genius had saved the day.

'The barge is going down!' said Rosetta. It slid off Superloo's top and sank like a stone, carrying all the remaining potties with it.

Like a tiny round boat, a single potty came bobbing to the shore – the only one that wasn't smashed or at the bottom of the river.

Rosetta picked it up. It was one of the fake potties all right. It had WALTER CLOSET stamped on the outside. She peered into it.

Rosetta was a tough girl, but even her hand flew to her mouth in shock. She showed it to Walter Closet. His face too went deathly pale.

'Villain!' he cried. 'What disrespect! What a scandal! What – what –!' He spluttered to a halt. No words could describe this outrage.

There was no doubt about it, the potties

would have caused a riot and people would have thought that he, Walter Closet, was to blame. The peelers would have locked him up and thrown away the key. If the crowd hadn't strung him up first.

'What is it? What's the matter?' cried Finn, seeing their horrified faces.

Rosetta passed him the potty. He peered inside. Painted right at the bottom, staring up at him, was a portrait of Queen Victoria. She looked like a scowling bulldog in a black widow's bonnet. She was not amused. And no wonder.

'Throw it back in the river!' declared Walter Closet angrily. 'What a frightful insult to our dear Queen!'

Finn was about to obey. But he suddenly remembered something. Just before they time travelled, Mr Lew Brush had asked for a potty baffle. Finn had no intention of touching something Victorian ladies tinkled through, but maybe this rude potty would do instead.

As all their eyes turned towards Superloo, Finn slipped the potty secretly under his jacket.

Superloo was fully emerged now. It came gliding gracefully towards the bank, floating, like a giant silver swan, on its fully inflated hover cushion.

'Hi, Superloo!' yelled Finn, waving and rushing towards it. He ignored Lord Gripper and his hired thugs, flailing about in the water. They didn't seem dangerous now.

The great toilet genius came sliding up the bank on its airbag.

Its cubicle door swished open.

'Hi, you guys!' came a chirpy voice from inside. 'Anyone like a lift to the railway station?'

Finn nipped in first. '*Pssst!*' he said to Superloo. 'Open your storage compartment. I've got a potty to take back for Mr Brush.'

For once, Superloo obeyed without arguing. A little door slid open in its silver wall. Finn stashed the potty safely inside.

'What about, "Oh, Superloo, I'm really pleased to see you"?' huffed the toilet, sounding hurt.

'Of course I'm pleased to see you!' said Finn. 'You're a hero! You foiled the evil potty plot.'

'Did I?' said the toilet. Then added quickly. 'It was easy-peasy for someone of MY brain power!' Even though it was sheer chance that it had popped up underneath the barge.

But where were Finn's Victorian friends? He poked his head out of the cubicle. 'Come on!' He beckoned to them. 'Don't be scared.'

Still, they hung back. Superloo opened its door wider as if to welcome them. As soon as Walter Closet saw Superloo's streamlined silver bowl and all its other toilet facilities, he was in.

'Astonishing!' he marvelled, his green eyes on stalks. 'Absolutely astonishing!'

'You ain't getting me in that contraption,' declared Snake. 'Anyhow, the potties is all destroyed. You don't need us no more.'

'Yes, we do,' said Finn. 'I don't trust that Lord Gripper. He might try something else.'

He and Snake exchanged glances. They both knew that Walter Closet was no match for the ruthless potty magnate. Lord Gripper could eat him for breakfast.

'And, anyhow, I would dearly like to see the Queen,' added Rosetta.

'Then we shall take the donkey cart,' said Snake, 'and meet you at the railway station.'

'Thanks,' said Finn. He felt better with Snake and Rosetta backing him up.

But there was no time to stand around talking. Lord Gripper and some of his thugs had reached the bank. They were scrambling out. Lord Gripper was shaking his fist. He looked really, really furious. What was he shouting? Better not to know.

'See you at the station,' said Finn as Snake and Rosetta rushed for the donkey cart.

'All aboard?' asked the toilet.

'Aye, aye, Captain,' grinned Finn.

The great toilet genius closed its door and launched itself on to the river again.

As Superloo sailed towards the railway station, back at the potty works Big Bertha was on her last legs.

The potty workers stood around, gaping, as more cracks appeared and ran, like jagged forked lightning, up and down her sides.

'Get back! She's going!' someone yelled.

Suddenly, with a mighty crash that made the whole factory shake, Big Bertha collapsed in clouds of dust.

The dust cleared. The workers stared in disbelief. They'd been slaves to that oven, sweating in its heat, stoking its fires, feeding it potties endlessly. But now it was just a steaming heap of bricks.

Someone raised a tiny cheer.

'Sixpence fine!' snapped a foreman.

No one took any notice. The cheer spread. Workers came out of the paint room and the glazing room and joined in. It grew louder until the whole dismal potty works was just one big *HURRAH*!

And the foremen couldn't do a single thing to stop it.

Just at that moment, Lord Gripper came staggering in the gate. He was dripping wet, slimy with riverweed and other more smelly things. Water snails slithered through his hair. In soggy boots he squelched up to the cheering workers.

He was in such a rage he hardly seemed to notice Big Bertha was gone.

'Get back to work!' he screamed, the veins in his forehead bulging like fat, red worms. 'Get back to work, you idle wretches! I'll have every one of you flogged!'

The cheering stopped. There was a deadly silence. 'Well!' shrieked Lord Gripper, frothing at the mouth like a mad dog. 'What are you waiting for?'

But the potty workers had tasted freedom. And they'd been so badly treated for so long. Suddenly, their mood turned ugly. A little boy, the poor weary runner from the drying room, pointed an accusing finger at Lord Gripper.

'He must pay!' he shrilled in his clear, childish voice, 'for all the evil he has done. All the misery he has caused!'

There was a roar of agreement from the workers. 'He must pay! He must pay!' they chanted.

For a moment Lord Gripper carried on ranting. 'I'll skin you alive!' He couldn't believe it. His potty workers were revolting! But then they surged forward. They were a shabby, half-starved bunch, but what he saw in their eyes scared him stiff. He couldn't reach his coach; the workers barred his way. So he turned tail and with his thugs behind him ran out of the gates.

The angry potty workers stared after him. It seemed their prey had escaped. Then one cried, 'After him!'

And they rushed in a howling mob through the streets.

CHAPTER TWELVE

'Full steam ahead!' quacked Superloo as it skimmed along the river on its airbag. It was having tremendous fun. 'Sailing is great!' it warbled. For once it didn't mind its ludicrous toilet body. On water it felt as light as a bubble.

It opened its cubicle door a crack and hailed a startled fisherman, 'Ahoy there, matey!'

The man stared, open-mouthed, at the great silver box cruising past. Then rowed, as fast as he could, back to shore.

'Will you stop messing about?' lectured Finn like a stern parent. 'You're not a ship. You're a toilet. Besides, you've got a guest.'

'*Whoops*, sorry,' said Superloo. 'How rude of me! You are Walter Closet, I believe, the esteemed toilet inventor? An honour, sir, to have you on board!'

Walter Closet looked around for a hand to shake. Finn didn't know how to start explaining.

'Look,' he said, 'I know this sounds really silly but we're from the future – where we have talking toilets.'

But there was no chance of keeping it simple when Superloo was listening.

'Actually,' it interrupted pompously, 'I am not just any old talking toilet. I am SUPERLOO! A fully automatic, time-travelling, self-cleaning public convenience. Oh, and I'm a genius too, of course.'

'How fascinating!' said Walter Closet. To Finn's surprise, he didn't seem in the least fazed. He thought toilets were capable of anything.

'Perhaps you would care to try out my flush?' Superloo asked Walter Closet. 'That button on the wall. Just wave your hand over it.'

Water swirled in the toilet bowl. Walter Closet listened, his eyes wide with wonder. Where was the clanking? The thunderous whoosh and gurgle, which even in his latest invention, the 1812 Overture Toilet, he hadn't been able to disguise? All you could hear was the softest *sssssss* like a tiny wave lapping on the shore.

He clasped his hands in ecstasy.

'A silent flush!' he whispered, in an awed voice. 'Sheer perfection! Oh, please, I beg of you, tell me the secret!'

You could practically hear Superloo preening itself. It just loved adoration. And, besides, a plan was forming in its cunning brain. It saw an easy way to get hold of its toilet ancestor.

'I will tell you,' said the toilet, 'in exchange for the 1812 Overture Toilet.'

Walter Closet considered Superloo's deal for a second. But only a second.

'Agreed!' he said. 'But the 1812 Overture Toilet must be presented to the Queen first. Then you shall have it, and gladly!'

He wasn't interested in it any more. His mind had moved on. He was already designing his next toilet in his head. With a silent flush, his loos would be famous. Everyone would want one. He would make a fortune!

He listened excitedly as Superloo explained about silent flushes.

Every so often he asked eager questions. Or cried out, 'Pure genius!'

Finn switched off. He always did that when toilet freaks got chatting. His mind drifted to thoughts of home.

I could murder a triple-cheese deep-crust pizza, he thought, his mouth watering. He knew there was one in the freezer. He hoped his big sister, the greedy pig, hadn't scoffed it.

He wouldn't have to wait long to find out. As soon as the ceremony at the station was over, they'd be whizzing back to the twenty-first century with, surprise, surprise, the 1812 Overture Toilet. He'd been sure they'd have to leave Superloo's relative behind.

He shook his head in amazement. You had to hand it to the wily toilet. It never stopped scheming. Somehow, it always got what it wanted.

A quacky voice broke into his thoughts. 'You two need a wash and brush up,' tutted Superloo fussily.

Finn didn't have to ask how it knew. From the second they'd stepped in the door, Superloo's many sensors had been feeding it data about its visitors. Its E-nose had analysed coal dust, clay dust, sweat and grime.

'You, Finn, especially, can't meet the Queen like that,' it scolded. 'You look like something the cat dragged in.'

Finn knew what was coming. 'Hang on!' he said. He ought to warn Walter Closet.

But there was no time. From the ceiling, warm-water jets hosed them down.

As the scummy water drained away, air played on them as if from a hundred hairdryers.

I hate this bit, thought Finn as a hot breeze blew up his unmentionables.

'Not the flowery scent!' pleaded Finn.

But Superloo was already spraying them with its Woodland Glade air freshener.

'That'll have to do,' said the toilet. 'We're almost there.'

Finn checked himself in Superloo's mirror. 'I hate the way your cleaning cycle gives me big hair! I look like a right prat!' He smoothed it down savagely.

'A cleaning cycle!' repeated Walter Closet. His flyaway hair was puffed out like a candyfloss cloud. For the first time in years his waistcoat had no food stains. 'Is there no end to this toilet's marvels?' he asked, amazed.

For once, Superloo passed up the chance to brag. It needed to concentrate. Using its sensors and brilliant brain, the great toilet genius was navigating its way up the riverbank and into the railway station through a disused tunnel.

Parp! A tiny trump came from its hover cushion as some air escaped.

Oh dear, thought the toilet. *I hope those water snails stay stuck on.* If they didn't, it could kiss goodbye to being a hoverloo. Its airbag would go flat as a pancake.

'Better not get too near Her Majesty,' said Finn, 'if you're going to make rude noises like that.'

'I don't plan to approach the Queen,' said the toilet. 'My appearance will only complicate matters. I shall stay out of sight. You, Finn, will attend the ceremony.' Here its voice sank to a whisper. 'And make sure Walter Closet sticks to his part of the deal.'

Finn glanced at Walter, but the inventor wasn't listening. He was dreaming of his next toilet design.

'I'm sure he will,' said Finn. Walter seemed like an honourable guy. Finn didn't mind going to the ceremony anyway. He'd like to get a glimpse of Queen Victoria before they left.

'Is she as miserable as people say?' asked Finn.

'Oh, more,' quacked Superloo, 'but it's not her fault really. She never got over the death of poor Prince Albert.'

Somewhere in the distance a silver band struck up 'God Save the Queen'.

'Oh no,' said Walter Closet. 'That's the royal train arriving! I should be on the platform with the welcoming committee.'

He leapt out of the cubicle. Finn followed. Behind them, Superloo closed its doors and switched off its lights to conserve energy. Now all it had to do was wait.

'Where are we?' asked Finn, staring around. His voice echoed in the dark tunnel. He stretched out an arm. 'Ugh!' His fingers touched black, slimy moss on the walls.

'The railway station is just ahead!' cried Walter Closet over his shoulder. And he hurried on towards the patch of sunlight at the end of the tunnel.

CHAPTER THIRTEEN

The Queen's train hadn't arrived – the band had only been practising – but it was due at any moment.

The mayor checked his watch. He felt like a nervous wreck. The town had never had a royal visit before and now the Queen herself was coming! It was an enormous honour, but also a massive headache.

'Please, please let nothing go wrong,' he whispered.

Waiting on the platform with him were all the town's toffs. Lady Gripper and the two Gripper children were among them. There was just one thought in Lady Gripper's head. It wasn't about her husband being chased to the station by an angry mob of potty workers – she didn't know about that yet. It wasn't even about meeting Her Majesty.

'I must pluck a rose!' she whispered in Miss Gripper's ear. 'Else I shall burst!'

Miss Gripper's sharp little weasel eyes had been searching about. *What is Pa up to?* she was thinking. Surely those fake potties should be here by now! Master Gripper had already squealed, 'Awwest Walter Closet! Flog him! Hang him high!' And she'd had to box his ears and hiss, '*Shush!* Not yet, you booby!'

'I'm bursting!' whispered Lady Gripper again. 'If I don't go NOW, I shall disgrace myself in front of Her Majesty!'

'Oh, Ma!' snapped Miss Gripper impatiently. 'Do stop making a fuss! There's a toilet right there. In front of you!'

She pointed to the great wardrobe, carved with crowns, which stood a little way down the platform.

'But that is the 1812 Overture Toilet!' said Lady Gripper. 'It is to be presented to the Queen!'

'*Pooh!*' said the spirited Miss Gripper. 'What of it? And, anyhow, no one is looking.'

Lady Gripper glanced quickly around. Her daughter was right. Everyone was peering down the track, craning their necks, looking out for the royal train.

And, in any case, thought Lady Gripper snootily, *in this town, I am as good as the Queen. Why should I not wee in her toilet?*

Besides, she couldn't wait a second longer. She flounced towards the wardrobe. Her bustle, as big as a wheelie bin, and her trailing bird of paradise feathers almost got trapped in the door, but she crammed herself inside.

She hadn't been there for Walter Closet's talk and demonstration. She'd been too busy swanning around the town in her coach, lording it over the common people, so she had no idea how the toilet worked. Or of the dangers of setting the music and the flush going together.

There was no problem at first. *La! How grand!* she thought as she settled herself on the fine mahogany seat of the crouching lion toilet bowl.

But, when it came to flushing, she looked round baffled. Should she pull that golden chain or push that lever? She'd never actually used a toilet before. Lord Gripper thought they were a cissy, modern fad. The mere mention of them drove him into a fury. At Gripper Towers, only potties were allowed.

Then she heard the band strike up 'God

Save the Queen'. Was this just another practice? Or was Her Majesty here at last? In a
panic, she leapt off the loo. Struggling to pull
up her bloomers, her big bustle whacked a
lever. Then she lost her balance, grabbed the
chain and fell back again on the seat. Suddenly,
all around her, things started to happen. As if
the toilet had come to life!

First, there was an ominous clanking, from
deep in the mechanism. Then a few deep,
throaty gurgles.

What is that? thought Lady Gripper, looking
round, terrified.

Then the flush really got going. With a tremendous *WHOOSH!* the water swirled round
the bowl. '*Ahhh!*' screeched Lady Gripper,
hanging on tight. The suck was so powerful it
seemed to be dragging her down!

At the same time the roars of *The 1812
Overture* cannon battered her ears. *BOOM!
BOOM!*

As Walter Closet had feared, the toilet's
mechanism couldn't stand the strain. Everything was jolting, jumping about. Screws and
bolts pinged out. Pipe joints loosened, then
broke. The 1812 Overture Toilet was shaking
itself to pieces.

'Help!' squawked Lady Gripper. But no one could hear her above the racket. She tried to heave herself off the toilet bowl. But her bustle was well and truly jammed.

BOOM! With a mighty crash, the last cannon sounded. It was the toilet's death knell.

Water from the cistern cascaded down; the wardrobe itself flew apart. Bits of toilet mechanism and porcelain scattered all over the platform. And there was Lady Gripper, dripping wet, sitting on the remains of the lion toilet bowl, with a stunned look on her face.

Finn and Walter Closet arrived just in time to see the toilet disintegrate. 'My toilet!' cried Walter Closet.

The mayor looked frantic. Now what would they present to Her Majesty?

But things were about to go even more pear-shaped.

As the VIPs struggled to free Lady Gripper's bustle from the toilet bowl, Master Gripper squealed out, 'Here is Pa!'

Lord Gripper came squelching in.

'*Pooh*, Pa!' said Miss Gripper, with her malicious grin. 'You smell like a sewer!'

Then, from outside the station, they heard angry roars.

'My potty workers are revolting!' barked Lord Gripper. 'The villains are after my hide!'

Everyone in the station could hear their howls. 'Give us Lord Gripper! Let us deal with the monster! He shall get what he deserves!'

The peelers were struggling to hold back the mob. The mayor was wringing his hands. What a sight for the Queen when her train pulled in! Lady Gripper, sitting on the toilet for all to see. And a howling mob of potty workers, baying for blood. The town would be shamed. It would never live it down.

And, to make matters worse, someone shouted, 'Here comes the royal train!' They could see it in the distance, glinting purple and gold – could see it puffing out steam. Why wasn't it coming closer? It had stopped, for some reason, about a mile down the track.

'Shoot the potty workers!' shrieked the gruesome Master Gripper, who was hoping for rivers of blood.

'Yes, peelers, fetch your firearms! Do your duty!' roared Lord Gripper.

'No!' came a ringing voice. It was Walter Closet. He strode forward. For once, he didn't look like a batty toilet inventor. Superloo's cleaning cycle had spruced him up no end. His shirt was sparkling white. His big hair streamed out like a lion's mane.

Wow, he looks, like, quite heroic! thought Finn.

Walter Closet's eyes blazed with anger. 'There will be no shooting here!' he cried. 'Let me go out and talk to them.'

'You!' snarled Lord Gripper, his lip curling in scorn. 'What can *you* do? They need shooting, every one, for daring to rise up against their master!'

'Yes, potty workers should know their place!' said Lady Gripper, who'd just been released from the toilet bowl. She came staggering up, her fine clothes in tatters.

'Oh my!' she cried, putting a hand to her head. 'I feel faint!'

She immediately swooned, sinking down on the platform. No one took the least notice.

But Walter Closet was already marching towards the station exit. Finn hurried alongside him. 'No,' said Walter, pushing him back. 'You stay here. It's too dangerous.'

When Walter saw the town square, even he

grew pale. The happy, cheering crowd had melted away, the flags had been trampled underfoot. Instead, there was a sea of raging potty workers. For a second he paused behind the thin line of peelers fighting to keep the mob back. It seemed hopeless. Even if he ventured out there, how could he get himself seen and heard?

'Sir! Sir!' yelled a familiar voice. A hand waved. 'Over 'ere!'

It was Rosetta with Snake in the donkey cart. Somehow, they'd found a clear space at the edge of the square. Walter slipped under the peelers' linked arms and thrust his way through the screaming crowd.

'I need somewhere high up,' he said, as he reached the cart. 'I wish to address the potty workers!'

'I knows the very place, sir,' said Snake, giving the donkey's reins a flick. 'Hop in!'

Meanwhile, just up the track, there was a crisis on the royal train. In the saloon sat a dumpy little woman, dressed from head to toe in black. She didn't look pleased. In fact, she looked like a bulldog that's swallowed a wasp.

'We must have a wee, immediately,' snapped Queen Victoria.

The royal saloon wasn't anything like a train carriage. It looked just like a Victorian living room, with velvet curtains, overstuffed sofas and loads of clutter. It also had a potty, disguised, of course, as something else.

The trouble was, it was so well disguised that no one could find it.

The Queen's lady-in-waiting scurried about, frantically searching. Where on earth was the potty hidden? Was it in the sewing basket? No. Was it disguised as a pile of books, a coal scuttle? She lifted up the sofa cushions. No, not there. She even looked in a potted fern.

'I am afraid, Your Majesty,' she said, 'they have forgot to put your potty on board.'

Queen Victoria pursed up her mouth. She looked even less pleased.

The lady-in-waiting made a timid suggestion.

'Is Your Majesty aware,' she said, 'that there is a toilet waiting on the platform? The 1812 Overture Toilet, I believe it is called. By all accounts it is modern, even revolutionary.'

'A revolutionary toilet?' said the Queen,

shocked. 'The Queen of England could never permit herself to use such an object! It would not be proper!'

On the other hand, she was desperate. Beneath her black crackly frock her legs were crossed.

What would Albert have done? she thought. When she had to make a difficult decision, she always asked herself that question. And the answer came immediately.

Dear Albert would not stand on ceremony, the Queen decided. And had he not once said, 'If I wasn't a prince, I would have been a plumber'? He had always been fascinated by new experimental drains and loos.

'We shall use this revolutionary toilet,' announced the Queen, with great dignity. 'Albert would have approved. Inform the mayor when we arrive. And tell our train driver to get a move on!'

As the royal train steamed into the station, Walter Closet was in the town square trying to calm the furious potty workers.

'Noble potty workers . . .' he began.

But his voice was drowned out by the cries and chanting of the mob.

Snake had, somehow, managed to steer the little donkey cart through the crowds.

'Climb up on Albert!' he'd said. 'So they can see and hear you!'

So Walter Closet had climbed Prince Albert's statue. He was standing on the plinth, by the legs of the prancing horse, but no one had noticed – the potty workers were all facing towards the station. He climbed higher, so now he was standing on the horse's bum, just behind the bronze prince.

'Noble potty workers!' he shouted again.

But still no one was listening. Suddenly Snake and Rosetta were on the plinth, yelling out for the crowd's attention.

'Dear friends!' called Rosetta, her high clear voice rising above the din. 'You know us!'

'Aye!' cried Snake. 'You call our pa a hero. Now listen to this man, for his sake!'

Many potty workers swivelled round. Some shushed the others. Walter Closet took a deep breath. It was now or never.

'Potty workers!' he cried in a loud and thrilling voice. 'I know you have been badly treated by a cruel master! I know your skills have not been appreciated!'

The angry cries stopped. Instead, there were growls of agreement from the crowd.

Walter Closet flung up an arm. His big hair glittered like a golden halo; his eyes shone with inspiration. Standing astride the horse's bum, he was an imposing figure. All were listening now. You could have heard a pin drop in the town square.

'I am here to tell you that Lord Gripper is finished! The old tyrant will never make another potty. Big Bertha has fallen down. That you know! But he has also engineered an evil potty plot . . .'

There were rumblings among the workers. Some knew about the potty plot. Some didn't. But what they *did* know was that they had lost their jobs. Even being a slave in Lord Gripper's factory was better than seeing your family starve.

But Walter Closet had a vision. His eyes blazing, he told the potty workers, 'Work for me! My factory needs you! I am going to design a new toilet. One with a silent flush. And, I tell you, it will conquer the world!'

He was really carried away now. The workers hung on his every word.

'Work for me!' he cried, his voice ringing

round the square. 'I promise you I will be a
fair and decent employer. No fines, no beatings,
shorter hours. And I shall pay you double what
Lord Gripper paid!'

'Did 'e say double?' muttered the potty
workers to each other. 'That's not bad!'

Should they trust this man? There was
something fine and honest about Walter
Closet, as he stood there behind Prince
Albert.

'Be part of my dream!' he cried. 'I cannot
do it without you. Let us go forward together
and build toilets with *pride*!'

'Hurrah!' cried the potty workers, throwing
their caps in the air.

Walter Closet wiped the sweat off his brow.
He felt more tired and more drained than he'd
ever done in his life. It had been a big ordeal
for the shy toilet inventor. He slid down from
the horse's bum.

'You've done it, sir!' said Snake, shaking his
hand. 'The potty workers are for you, every
man, woman and child!'

They'd even stopped shouting for Lord
Gripper's blood. Someone had cried, 'The
Queen is here!' Flags appeared from nowhere.
Someone else yelled, 'Good old Queen Vic!'

And suddenly the danger of a riot was over. Instead, the potty workers had decided to enjoy the holiday.

'Quick!' said Walter Closet. 'I must be there to greet the Queen!'

But this was easier said than done. The little donkey cart, with the three of them on board, could hardly force itself through the crowd. Everyone wanted to clap them on the back or shake them by the hand.

No one noticed the splendid coach, rumbling away from the station. It had the whole Gripper family inside.

'Whip them horses harder, else I'll whip you!' growled Lord Gripper out of the window to the driver.

'We're finished in this town,' he snarled at his family. 'Time to pack up and move on.'

'We're ruined!' shrieked Lady Gripper. 'We shall be in the Workhouse!'

'Ma's fainted again,' declared Master Gripper in a bored voice, picking at a scab on his knee.

'Are we really ruined, Pa?' asked Miss Gripper, with her sly, cruel grin.

'Us, missy?' roared Lord Gripper, his two dog's teeth gleaming. 'I should say not! We

Grippers will rise again, you have my word on it!'

And, with the horses galloping at full speed, their flanks foaming, the coach thundered up the hill to Gripper Towers.

CHAPTER FOURTEEN

Inside the station, there was big trouble.

The royal train, glittering purple and gold, was steaming up to the platform, the silver band was playing 'God Save the Queen', but the town mayor was gnawing his knuckles. 'We have no loo to present to Her Majesty!'

If he thought things couldn't get any worse, he was wrong.

For when the train stopped, it wasn't the Queen who got out first, but her lady-in-waiting. She had a discreet word in the mayor's ear: 'Her Majesty would like to pluck a rose.'

'More problems!' the mayor burst out, when the lady-in-waiting had climbed back on board. 'Her Majesty needs a wee! And we have nothing for her to wee in.'

The 1812 Overture Toilet was a wreck. They couldn't possibly take her to the nearest public conveniences.

'It's a disaster!' cried the mayor, almost tearing his hair out. 'Where, oh, where, can we find a toilet posh enough for the Queen?'

The town toffs stared at each other in dismay. Then Finn stepped forward. 'Sir,' he said to the mayor, 'I know of such a toilet –'

The mayor looked down. 'Begone!' he barked. 'Peeler, take this boy outside!'

A sturdy policeman stepped forward to grab Finn. But then Walter Closet rushed into the station, followed by Snake and Rosetta. They'd finally managed to make their way through the cheering crowd.

'Leave that boy alone!' snapped Walter Closet. 'He's with me! As are these two children!'

In a gabble of words, Finn explained the crisis to the toilet inventor. 'We must fetch Superloo,' he finished.

Walter Closet nodded. 'An excellent plan!'

Superloo, in all its shining silver glory, with its silent flush and other amazing technology, was a toilet not even a Queen would sniff at.

Walter Closet spoke a few words to the mayor. Then he and Finn hurried off.

They found Superloo where they'd left it – lurking in the dark railway tunnel.

Its sensors told it they were coming. It opened its cubicle door wide. 'Have you got my famous relative?' it quacked. 'I can't wait to meet it!'

Finn skidded to a halt. *Whoops,* he thought.

In the panic over the Queen's bursting bladder, he'd forgotten about the 1812 Overture Toilet and the deal made between Superloo and Walter Closet.

'I fear,' said Walter, shaking his head sadly, 'that my toilet was destroyed by Lady Gripper when she set the flush and the music going at the same time.'

'*Noooooo!*' Superloo gave a great wail of grief.

Finn glanced at Walter Closet. 'Stay out here for a minute,' he told him. 'Better leave this to me.'

Finn stepped inside the cubicle. No one knew Superloo's moods better than he did. He knew the great toilet genius was genuinely upset about its lost toilet relative, but it was a drama queen too. It would milk this situation for all it was worth.

'My poor toilet relative!' cried Superloo. Its tinny robot voice broke into heart-rending sobs. 'I know it was primitive. I know it was thick as two short planks! But it was very precious. Not least, because it evolved into ME!'

'Yes, yes, yes,' said Finn impatiently. He'd heard all this before. He felt sorry for Superloo, but they hadn't much time. How long could the Queen's bladder hold out?

'I'm so *lonely*!' sobbed Superloo. 'You, Finn, have family! What do I have? Nothing. Not even my relative! It is so, so hard being a toilet genius.'

Finn didn't want to get involved in those discussions. They could be here all day. He had to find some way to persuade the toilet and fast.

You could always count on one thing working – appealing to Superloo's vanity, its giant ego.

'The Queen of England needs you!' Finn cried. 'She desperately wants a wee.'

'Does she?' said Superloo, sounding interested.

'And only you, Superloo, are grand enough,' said Finn.

'That's true,' Superloo agreed.

It had a think. Usually, it didn't let people use it as a toilet – the very idea was an insult.

'The Queen only wants a tiny tinkle,' Finn coaxed the toilet.

'*Hummm*,' said Superloo. It was tempted. It was an honour really – a royal bum on its toilet bowl. Superloo was a terrible snob. It just couldn't resist.

'I'll do it!' it cried, instantly recovering from the loss of its toilet relative. 'For Queen and Country!'

'Good old Superloo,' said Finn. 'You've saved the day again!'

With Superloo hovering behind them, Walter Closet and Finn went rushing back to the platform. The VIPs looked alarmed as the great silver cubicle floated by and settled itself next to the royal train.

Walter Closet tried to reassure them: 'This toilet has no equal! Her Majesty could not want for anything better!'

It was too late anyway. Victoria couldn't wait any longer. She came dashing out.

Smoothly, Superloo opened its door for her. Victoria shot inside. The door slid shut. Superloo's BUSY sign lit up.

What was going on in there? Everyone on the platform waited, hardly daring to breathe. Would the Queen like the toilet? She was well known for being very hard to please.

Finn was more worried than the rest.

I hope Superloo doesn't speak, he was thinking. *It'll scare the life out of her.*

But, for once, it seemed, Superloo was perfectly behaved. After ten minutes, the door opened again. The tiny, dumpy Queen came trotting out. And, wonder of wonders, she was smiling!

'Gentlemen,' she said to the town toffs. 'We have seldom been so delighted. Where is the maker of this magnificent toilet?'

Finn pushed Walter Closet forward. He began to protest, 'I did not make it, Your Maj–' but Finn kicked his ankle. In any case, the Queen wasn't listening.

'We entirely approve of your toilet,' she said. 'Especially the silent flush. We shall order several for Buckingham Palace.'

'Your Majesty,' stammered Walter Closet. 'I shall make them with all speed.'

'From henceforth,' trilled Victoria. 'You may call yourself, Walter Closet, toilet maker by Royal Appointment.'

'Your Majesty,' said Walter with a deep bow as she clambered back on to her train.

The silver band was crashing out 'God Save the Queen'. Outside, the potty workers were cheering their loudest. The train got up steam. Victoria, still smiling, waved regally out of the window.

Rosetta and Snake waved back. They'd never dreamt they'd be this close to Her Majesty. Snake wished he didn't look so filthy. He scrubbed some soot off his face with spit. 'God save our dear old Queen!' he cried.

The mayor mopped his brow. *Phew, she's leaving*, he thought. Thanks to Walter Closet, they had avoided disaster by a whisker.

But the royal train didn't budge. Instead, a lady-in-waiting pulled down a window. The Queen leant out.

'Boy, come here!' she commanded. She was beckoning to Snake.

Oh no, thought the mayor. *What's he done to annoy Her Majesty?* Perhaps it was his ragged, dirty appearance that had offended her.

'Approach, boy!' ordered the Queen. Snake seemed strangely reluctant, so the mayor hustled him up to the train window.

'I know you,' said the Queen, forgetting to use the royal 'we'. The mayor gasped in amazement. How did the Queen of England know a common climbing boy?

'I was at a window when you came to Buckingham Palace,' the Queen continued. 'It was in winter, several years ago, before my dear Albert passed away.'

Even more peculiar, the mayor thought, amazed. What had this boy been doing at Buckingham Palace?

Snake swallowed hard. He knew exactly what he'd been doing – nicking ice from the ornamental ponds. He was for it now. Could they hang you for stealing ice? In Victorian England, kids had been hanged for stealing handkerchiefs.

But the Queen was still smiling, although a tear glittered in her eye. 'You saved my dear Albert,' she said.

'What?' said Snake. 'I means, beg your pardon, ma'am?'

Then he remembered. There'd been a great pond, frozen over, with a fountain in the middle. Some guy had appeared from nowhere and tried to skate on it. The ice had cracked underneath him and he'd fallen through. Snake had pulled him out, then hopped it when other people came running. He'd had no idea it was the Prince.

'Were it not for you,' said Victoria, 'my Albert would have drowned that day. And we should have been parted even sooner.'

She dabbed at her eyes with a lacy hanky.

Snake scuffled his feet and squirmed with embarrassment. He had no idea what to say.

'I must reward you,' declared Queen Victoria, 'for your noble deed. But what to give you? What would Albert do, I wonder?'

Snake mumbled, 'I wants nothing, Your Majesty.'

Walter Closet stepped forward. He made a deep bow. 'Ma'am,' he said, 'this boy's family are in desperate circumstances. His mother is dead. His father was badly hurt in an accident. And he and his sister must work as a climbing boy and slavey.'

'What, they do not go to school?' said the Queen.

'School?' echoed Snake. 'I ain't never been to school.' Neither he nor Rosetta could read or write.

Suddenly Victoria knew what she must do.

Albert had been a big fan of education. 'I shall send my own doctors to cure his father. Then I shall pay his father a pension for life, so his children may go to school and need not work.'

'Most generous, ma'am,' said the mayor.

Victoria looked pleased with herself. Dear Albert, even though he was dead, always told her the right thing to do.

'Oh, and Lord Mayor,' she said graciously, 'we shall donate another statue of our dear Albert to the town.'

'Most generous again, ma'am,' grovelled the mayor, while privately thinking, *Not another blooming statue of Albert! Where on earth are we going to stick it?*

The Queen waved again as everyone applauded. Her smile made her look pretty, almost girlish.

'We have been much pleased by our visit here!' was the last thing they heard her say.

Phew, thought the mayor as the train started to move. Was she going at last? He felt weak from the strain, but, despite all his fears, the visit had been a big success. And the Grippers seemed to have scarpered. *I hope it's for good,* thought the mayor. He'd never liked that brute, Lord Gripper, who acted like he owned the town.

The potty workers were surging into the station, not to riot, but to get a glimpse of the Queen. She steamed away, to the cheers of the crowd and the clashing din of the town's silver band.

'Potty workers!' Walter Closet was shouting. 'Tomorrow we start work. We have toilets to make for Her Majesty!'

Finn was standing apart from the crowd. Walter Closet, Snake and Rosetta were talking excitedly. Rosetta threw off her slavey's cap and trampled on it. Snake's sooty face had the biggest grin in the world. 'Wait until Pa hears!' he was saying. Finn smiled too. He just knew those two would be all right – they could take care of themselves.

Time to go home, he thought. He was feeling really homesick for the twenty-first century.

Only he noticed a great juicy raspberry sound coming from Superloo's airbag. *PARP!* It was a good job the Queen was well out of earshot.

'What's happening?' cried Finn, rushing into the cubicle.

'My hover cushion's deflating again,' quacked

the great toilet genius. The water snails who'd plugged the puncture were slithering away, leaving silvery trails across the platform.

PARRRRP! It deflated some more.

'I'm not mobile any more,' mourned Superloo with a sniffle. 'I'm so depressed.'

'For heaven's sake!' said Finn. The last thing he wanted was the great toilet genius going into one of its sulks where it switched off its lights and wouldn't communicate.

'What's it matter, if you can't cross a few metres of floor?' argued Finn. 'You can travel through centuries! You're like a Time Lord!'

'You're right!' said Superloo, instantly bouncy again. 'Only I'm better than them! They don't have my silent flush and self-cleaning facilities and jumbo bog-roll holder!'

'I want my tea,' said Finn, thinking of that triple-cheese pizza. 'Can we go now?'

'Yes, we must,' said Superloo, whose power was getting lower by the minute. If it didn't go now, it wouldn't have the energy for the return trip.

'Hang on a sec,' said Finn, just before Superloo closed its door. Rosetta and Snake had turned round; they were waving at him!

Finn waved back. He didn't want to make a big deal about it or have a soppy farewell. It was better to just slip away. They didn't know he was leaving for good, going back to the future. They had no idea of Superloo's powers.

But Walter Closet did. He left the happy throng and came over.

'We're off now,' said Finn.

Walter Closet shook his head. 'I can hardly believe it,' he said. 'This has been the greatest day of my life. Meeting this incredible toilet, and the Queen. And, of course, you, Finn.'

The toilet inventor shook Finn's hand. 'When you have both gone,' he said. 'I shall think it was all a dream.'

'No, you won't,' said Superloo, its voice drawling slightly as its energy levels slumped. 'Take something as a souvenir.'

'A souvenir?' said Walter Closet. 'Are you sure?'

He came inside, looked around the smooth silver walls. What could he take? Everything was so streamlined. The toilet bowl and hand washing facilities were built in and the clock and mirror were screwed to the wall. Then he noticed the toilet roll. He hadn't seen it before, hidden inside its holder.

'What's that?' he asked, pulling out a few sheets of dimpled tissue.

'It's toilet paper,' Finn told him, 'for wiping your bum on. Haven't you seen it before?'

'No,' Walter Closet shook his head. 'What a brilliant idea!' People in Victorian times used rags or pieces of newspaper. 'May I really take it?' he asked, in an awed voice.

'Feel free!' said Superloo. 'But we must go now.' Its power was dangerously low.

'Goodbye,' said Walter Closet. 'Today has changed my life. You have taught me so much about toilets.'

And he left the cubicle, proudly carrying his bog-roll souvenir. He was already planning, in his head, how to make his own.

Months later, when he delivered the silent flush toilets to Buckingham Palace, they came with a free gift. A year's supply of toilet rolls for the Queen's personal use. The Queen was delighted with Walter Closet's latest invention. 'So soft and kind to our royal posterior,' she told her lady-in-waiting.

'The man is a genius,' she told her prime minister. 'We don't know where he gets his ideas from! He shall be knighted in our next honours list!'

And that's how a humble Victorian gardener's boy ended up as *Sir* Walter Closet.

CHAPTER FIFTEEN

'We've landed!' cried Superloo. 'We're back home!'

Finn slid down off the silver walls. He stumbled to his feet. 'I just hate time travelling.'

'Yes, yes, yes,' quacked Superloo, as if it had heard all this before. It opened its cubicle door. It couldn't wait to meet Mr Lew Brush and tell him all about their Victorian adventure – the thrills, the triumphs, the tears.

'It was sad we didn't rescue your toilet relative,' said Finn, 'and that it shook itself to bits.'

'Well, you win some, you lose some,' said Superloo. It gave a sob as if to say, 'I'm really gutted.' But then it suddenly perked up. 'Look on the bright side!' it boomed. 'It meant Queen Victoria used little ME instead! It is a moment I shall always treasure.'

'And another good thing,' added Finn, 'we saved Walter from the evil potty plot, didn't we?'

'Yes, we did!' agreed Superloo. 'Finn, you were great out there. I was proud of you.'

'Really?' said Finn, embarrassed but tickled pink. The great toilet genius seldom praised anyone but itself. If it said, 'You were great, Finn,' it meant it.

Superloo slid open its cubicle door. Finn staggered out. 'We're in the jungle!' he called back in a panic.

'Oh dear,' tutted the toilet. 'Have I made a slight miscalculation?'

'It's OK!' said Finn, suddenly realizing where they were. This wasn't jungle, after all. They'd landed among tall, tangled pea plants. Mr Brush's allotment shed was just over there.

Finn rushed towards it. He was desperate to get out of these itchy Victorian unmention-ables, back into his jeans and T-shirt. He spat on his hands and plastered his hair close to his skull. He couldn't go out on to the twenty-first-century streets with big hair. What if any of his mates saw him?

He dashed inside. 'Mr Brush! Blaster! We're back! Where are you, Mr Brush? I've brought you a potty!'

No one answered. But there, slap bang in the middle of Mr Brush's cosy shed home, was another public convenience.

Finn did a double take. He thought, bewildered, *What's that doing there?* It was just like Superloo, from the outside anyway – the same shiny metal walls, the same signs: FREE, BUSY, CLEANING.

But did it have a brain, like the great toilet genius?

'Hiya,' Finn greeted the toilet. 'How're you doing?'

No quacky voice answered back. The cubicle door stayed firmly shut. If the loo *did* have a brain, it wasn't talking.

Finn snatched his twenty-first-century clothes off the shed floor and put them on. That was better. He felt like himself again.

'Mr Brush?' he called. Where was he? Maybe he could shed some light on this new loo.

'*Aaaargh!*'

A strangled cry came from among the pea sticks. Finn rushed outside. He saw Superloo being hoisted high in the air by a big yellow crane on the back of a lorry.

'Put me down IMMEDIATELY!' protested Superloo. It was so undignified for a great toilet genius to be dangling in mid-air.

A familiar sad, baggy face peered out of the cab.

'Blaster?' said Finn. Surely the crumbling old hound wasn't driving the lorry?

But then Mr Lew Brush's head poked out.

'It's all right, Finn, it's only me. Sorry, Superloo!' he shouted to the dangling toilet. 'We've got no choice. We've got to move fast, find another place for you to hide.'

Superloo would have liked to argue. It didn't like it at all, being bossed about by humans, but its power levels were in the red danger zone. Its voice came again, 'I – must – protest!' but faintly, as if from the bottom of a deep well.

'Hop in, Finn,' said Mr Lew Brush. He shifted a few levers. Superloo swayed in mid-air, then came down with a bump on the back of the lorry. There was a muffled squawk of protest, then silence.

'It needs to recharge,' said Finn as Blaster slobbered on his hand in welcome.

'It can in a minute,' said Mr Lew Brush. 'Don't worry.'

'But where are we going?' asked Finn.

'You'll soon see,' said Mr Lew Brush as they jolted along the bumpy track out of the allotments.

'And where did you get this crane?' asked Finn. Mr Lew Brush had a bright yellow jacket, with HIGHWAY MAINTENANCE on the back.

'*Errrrr*, I borrowed it,' answered Mr Lew Brush vaguely. 'It was just parked by some roadworks, doing nothing.'

Finn sighed. Better not ask any more questions. The old wartime spy had all kinds of tricks up his sleeve. Anyway, Finn didn't much care if Mr Lew Brush had done something dodgy. As long as Superloo was saved from the toilet terminators.

They were in town now. Driving through the busy streets and right into the middle of the town square.

There's Prince Albert's statue! thought Finn.

The last time he'd seen that, he'd been back in Victorian times.

'Just look official,' said Mr Lew Brush as he leapt out of the cab. They were in a corner of the square, away from the crowds. Mr Lew Brush said, 'Here, give me a hand. We've got to shift this sheet of metal.'

Underneath the sheet was a hole, with pipes and wires packed inside.

'Now I know where that other loo came from,' said Finn. 'The one in your shed. You

175

nicked it from here, didn't you? And you're going to put Superloo in its place.'

'Spot on!' said Mr Lew Brush. 'I thought, *Where's the last place they'll look for Superloo?* Right where a toilet ought to be, that's where!'

Finn shook his head in admiration. The great toilet genius should be grateful, having Mr Lew Brush on its side, but it'd probably only complain. Once it got back enough power to talk, that is.

Mr Brush was operating switches and levers, carefully lowering Superloo from the back of the lorry into the hole. There it could connect up with a power supply and water and sewage pipes too, if it wanted.

'Right!' said Mr Lew Brush. 'All we have to do now is wait.'

They climbed back into the lorry.

'That other toilet,' Finn asked Mr Lew Brush, 'the one in your shed. I suppose it's not like Superloo, is it? I mean, does it have a brain?'

'Unfortunately not,' said Mr Lew Brush, who knew as well as Finn how Superloo longed for a soulmate. 'It's just a bog-standard loo, I'm afraid. Like all the rest.'

'Superloo's opening its doors,' said Finn. They climbed out of the cab. The toilet had obviously recharged. It was its usual bolshy self.

'I have never,' it huffed, 'been more humiliated! I who was sat upon by a royal bum! Tinkled in by Queen Victoria herself!'

'*Shush*, shut your door,' said Mr Lew Brush as he, Finn and Blaster crowded inside the cubicle. 'Flash up your BUSY sign. Just behave like an ordinary loo.'

'An ORDINARY loo!' yelped Superloo, outraged.

'It's only for the time being,' soothed Mr Brush. 'Until I find somewhere else for us to go. The allotments aren't safe any more. There was a bin van there this morning that shouldn't have been there, and someone searched my shed. I think they've tracked you down again.'

'I'm tired of running,' shouted Superloo wildly. 'It's time to turn and fight! Let me at these toilet-hunting scumbags! These ghouls who want my brain! I'll teach them a lesson they won't forget in a hurry!'

'Not this time,' said Mr Lew Brush. 'We don't even know who they are. And, anyway, I've left a decoy in my shed. That'll put them off the scent for a bit, buy us some time.'

Even as he spoke, back at the allotments, the three ninja assassins were sneaking back for a second search. They were determined to get their toilet – or die in the attempt.

Like tightrope walkers, they ran lightly along the top of the fence, then soared over the cabbage patch, in one graceful gazelle-like bound. Except for Dung Beetle, who misjudged the distance and dive-bombed into the compost heap. Two legs stuck out, waving wildly.

'*Paa!*' said Dung Beetle as he struggled free, spitting out horse manure.

He crept forward on shaky legs. He should have felt brave. After all, wasn't he a hero? Hadn't he knocked some guy's head off with a single karate blow? But that spirit dog had been really scary – a giant hound as big as a house, breathing fire like a dragon, with blazing eyes!

But, once again, it seemed luck was on his side. Dung Beetle twirled to the door of Mr Brush's shed. He sometimes wondered, *Why can't we just* walk? But ninjas never do things the easy way.

Feeling giddy from all that twirling, he sneaked a look inside. His heart was hammering, but no spirit dog came leaping out. Instead, the ninja apprentice gave a great '*Ha!*' of surprise.

Wildcat and Cobra backflipped over. Dung Beetle pointed a trembling finger. There was the toilet! He gabbled excitedly to the other two. It hadn't been there before, but they'd been shown pictures – it looked exactly like the loo they'd been sent to find.

In no time at all they'd loaded it into the bin van. It would be flown to a secret location, where top scientists would extract its four-billion-dollar microchip brain.

The bin van lumbered off.

'You have done well, young Dung Beetle,' said Cobra with a solemn nod. 'For a second time, you have proved yourself.'

'When we return,' said Wildcat, 'you shall be an apprentice no longer, but a fully qualified ninja warrior!'

Back in the town square, for a short time Superloo had been left alone. Finn had gone rushing off for his tea, and Mr Lew Brush, taking Blaster with him, was driving the borrowed crane back to where it belonged.

He'd been over the moon about his potty, the one with Queen Vic's face on the *inside*.

'And you say this is the only one in existence?' he'd asked Finn. 'I shall treasure it always!'

He didn't even mind about the potty baffle.

'Oh, you can pick them up easily in junk shops,' he'd told Finn. 'You know they look like big lace doilies, with beads round the edge? Well, many ladies mistake them for milk-jug covers.'

'*Yuk*, how gross!' Finn had said. But then he'd remembered: 'My gran's got one of those!'

How could he tell Gran, when she brought out her posh china tea set, that her milk-jug cover had been peed through by Victorian ladies?

'Better keep quiet about that,' Mr Lew Brush had advised. 'What she doesn't know won't hurt her.'

Mr Lew Brush would be back soon. He and Superloo had serious things to discuss – like where the great toilet genius could be safe from its pursuers.

The future looked uncertain, but Superloo

wasn't worried. Its brilliant brain would work something out.

Someone banged on the cubicle door.

'Whoever you are in there, will you hurry up?' cried a lady's voice from outside. 'I've been waiting ages!'

'Go away!' shouted Superloo rudely. 'Why do you think my BUSY sign is flashing? I do NOT want to be disturbed! I'm thinking!'

The startled lady scurried off to find another public convenience.

'Can't these humans ever leave me alone?' sighed Superloo to itself. 'They're always pestering me.'

It wouldn't admit that it was already missing Finn. It flushed its toilet bowl a few times. It always did that when it felt bored and lonely.

It was just about to play 'Drip, Drip, Drop Little April Showers', but there was no need because, suddenly, it felt cheery again.

'Wow!' it warbled to itself. 'Fantastic!'

Its super-bright brain, surfing historical websites, had found its next mission. Another ancient toilet that needed rescuing.

'I must tell Finn!' it quacked excitedly.

But, hang on, Finn had said as he left the cubicle, 'I've had it up to here with these rescue missions! It's way too much stress. I don't mind coming round for a chat, but no more trips into the past. Right? Absolutely, definitely. NO MORE!'

The toilet should have felt downhearted. Could this spell the end of their time-travel adventures? But Superloo pooh-poohed the idea.

'*Cha!*' the great toilet genius scoffed. 'Finn's such a silly sausage! He *always* says that. After every trip. But he doesn't *really* mean it. Not when he and I make such a cracking team!'

TOILET GAZETTE

2d

WHAT HAPPENED BACK IN VICTORIAN TIMES?

Snake and Rosetta managed Sir Walter Closet's business, while he invented even more amazing toilets.

Lord Gripper opened a new potty factory in Australia.

Pa retired to the country with Lizzie and Mr Bain's old donkey.

POTTY PUZZLE

Queen Victoria is desperate!
Can you get through the maze
to help her?

QUEEN VIC'S
ROYAL WORD SEARCH

Can you find these words in the grid below?

CHIMNEY	RAILWAY	FACTORY
SWEEP	OVERTURE	VICTORIAN
COACH	STATUE	

```
V  G  S  Z  H  M  N  C  V  C
C  J  I  W  L  H  Y  O  F  H
M  O  O  P  E  M  O  A  L  I
U  L  N  V  J  E  C  C  F  M
E  P  L  Z  E  T  P  H  W  N
V  I  C  T  O  R  I  A  N  E
P  Q  G  R  T  A  T  Q  Q  Y
W  N  Y  S  T  A  T  U  E  X
Y  A  W  L  I  A  R  L  R  P
C  H  J  B  K  K  W  B  E  E
```

AND THE NEXT STATION IS ...

Where is the royal train going?

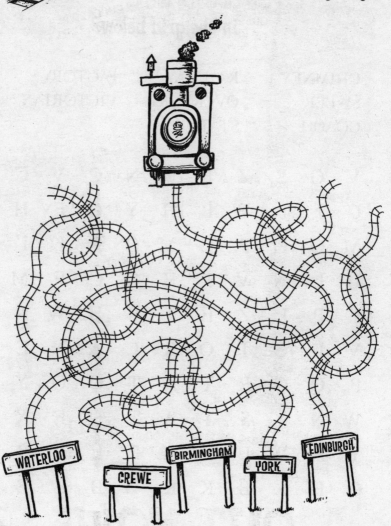

Join **SUPERLOO**

for more crazy missions into the past . . .

WILL SUPERLOO AND FINN SUCCEED IN THEIR QUEST TO FIND THE LEGENDARY TOILET OF KING TUTANKHAMUN?

SUPERLOO AND FINN ARE IN ROMAN BRITAIN WHERE THEY FIND GLADIATORS, BEARS . . . AND, OF COURSE, HADRIAN'S FAMOUS LATRINE!

SUPERLOO GETS KIDNAPPED – TUDOR STYLE! CAN FINN SAVE THE DAY?

A ROLLICKING RIDE TO VICTORIAN TIMES, INVOLVING SLUMS, AN EVIL FACTORY OWNER – AND THE QUEEN HERSELF!

OUT NOW!

puffin.co.uk